Love Grows
Stronger in Death

Love Grows Stronger in Death
Short Stories

Curated by:
Tope Akintayo

Edited by:
Ibrahim Babatunde Ibrahim
Basit Jamiu

Content

The Good Spirits

CHINUZOKE CHINUWA

Who is to say it is too late to be insane, to believe that the faulty tubes on the ceiling of this dead room can give me the light I need to reach you? I hate to say this, but your memories are withered, and my dread of our end is too much to bear. This is the first time the spirit barrier is out of my sight, and it means only one thing. I fear for our continuity now that the demons have killed you for the umpteenth time. There are cosmic laws written on my airy bones, seethed in my quantic expanse, and this is one of them: We cannot escape the Abyss after so many deaths at the hands of its minions.

But I believe that talking to you, regardless of our end, or pretending that you can hear me, is the only way to reach you before the interment, before Transcendence, when we cannot catch the faintest light. I must pretend that I have enough light to penetrate your death and feel you. I promised not to sit in silence should we come to our end, so listen to me, let me tell you about us. You will tell this story, too, because you speak as I speak. If you think about it, no one is more inclined to listen to a story than those who tell it. Stay in this small light with me, my dearest. Let me help you remember what matters.

~

That Sunday morning, before you died, you took a long walk to Old Park, hoping to escape infuriating boredom, having argued all week with your parents about your two-month absence from the church. You sat under a mango tree overlooking the park that reminded you of a time you felt most alive. When you were a little child, playing hide-and-seek with your mates in the cornfields that once covered the area, running after the ice cream truck on weekend evenings as it left your neighbourhood.

Your mother later called and said she was going to the church on the hill and wanted to be sure you were there with your father.

"No, the other church...the one in the valley," you lied as you untied your shoelaces, watching a pigeon perched on a mango tree branch. You could have been in Sunday school, teaching the lesson, but there you were under a tree, getting ideas you hoped you could use for the next school play, watching birds glide over a trimmed field, where men played soccer seemingly with no awareness of how their shirtless forms gleamed in the morning light.

As you relaxed in the shade of the tree, you saw two nuns walk past the shops across the street and imagined being a Catholic missionary somewhere far from the small town you had never left. As sharp sunlight bounced off a passing truck's windshield, you closed your eyes and saw yourself at the makeshift pulpit, two feet above the translator. The tiny chapel made of bamboo stood in the middle of a clearing, amid the well-spaced trunks of a huge banyan tree. Towering cocoyam plants with leaves like open umbrellas lined the longer sides of the rectangular hut.

A ball whizzed past your head, ending that imagination of life as a Catholic missionary, and your sight of the man who kicked the ball stirred further imagination. He wore black, white-rimmed shorts and a red, long-sleeved Liverpool jersey. He hurried over to the tree and apologised, resembling your boyfriend Kanim as he smiled and winked. He reminded you of a photograph of your father as a young man. Resemblance and recognition always seemed strange to you, as strange as time, but everything strange in this world is known to us.

~

That Sunday morning, before you died, you pictured your father in the congregation of the church on the hill. You pictured his chin raised as if to ensure unwavering attention to the speaker. Your father whose smile everyone said you had. Your father who was too concerned about the permanence of his faith, to have even the slightest regard for your scepticism and interest in the arts. So, it was easy to separate yourself from home since you thought of it as a box that moved from one place to another, from one generation to the next.

You never fit into that box—no box could contain you. Your consciousness is the apex of paradoxes, unpredictable but rightly so. That was why I sometimes struggled to find you in the Afterlife. One time, I was busy searching a very distant realm, so certain you had been reborn there, I forgot you wanted to visit a world in Andromeda and wondered why we had to travel so far to share a new lifeform. You told me that travelling farther for your rebirth did not necessarily exclude the worlds closest to this one, that we could visit the neighbouring realms to learn what they knew about Earth and what they hoped for it. I could not tell what it was about life on Earth that made you visit so often even though it was not the safest world in the mortal realms. But I see it now, my dearest. The truth that is so simple and yet so complex: There is no world like this one.

~

That Sunday morning, just before you died, you saw a man in ragged clothes as you walked by a fleet of trailers parked on the north stretch of Train B Road. You halted as you realised that he was waving at you, feeling apprehensive because he had bloodshot eyes. He crossed the first lane from the other side of the road and stood on the middle block. You half expected him to cross the second lane and ask you for directions, but he just stood there watching you.

As you moved to turn and keep walking, he raised a hand to his mouth twice. He barely whispered; no vehicles had passed but the noise would not have deterred your comprehension. He was hungry and he needed your help to get food, but you only had just enough money to take the bus down to the valley, to your boyfriend Kanim's backhouse—that tiny but magnificent sanctuary, as you once described it.

There was a rapture you could not shake off about that backhouse and the yard in which it stood. The breezy energy you had in the orchard and the garden; the pride when the peppers and tomatoes began to ripen; the scent of the morning glories before they folded at dusk; how the cathedral bells looked like the hibiscuses; how the Aloe vera grew among the pineapples as if they, too, were fruits.

Do you remember when you first met Kanim? Or when you kissed his torso for the first time, your fingers slithering down to his quivering groin as the lawn beneath the citrus trees turned into the softest bed you had ever laid on? Kanim with his dark skin glinting in the evening light, his whole form so stunning as if to be a breathing crystal through which you could view yourself. Kanim with his beards that smelled like scented dew on freshly trimmed grass, his nipples a breath away from your lips like mountains awaiting the kiss of a god. Kanim, whose angst and sexual desire found yours. Kanim with his falsetto laugh and his playful smirk. Kanim who helped you see colours when your mind drifted into gloom, whom you learned to see with your third eye even though you did not know it.

~

Before you died, you anticipated a good time at the backhouse. But you never made it there as it was too late when that man with bloodshot eyes crossed the road, running towards you. You turned to quicken your pace and bumped into two men who had appeared out of nowhere, then you turned to see the one behind you, who had waved earlier, now standing next to a fourth man. They all looked very alike—exact duplicates of each other—tall and sturdy, even the one in ragged clothes. The other three

4

reminded you of the *Men in Black* as they wore black suits and black shoes as if dressed for a funeral. They looked down on you with a weirdly distant but directly menacing sight, and their bloodshot eyes bulged and thinned and widened, skin and flesh tearing and folding into red scales, huge reptilian eyes glaring at you. One of them opened his mouth and hissed, revealing a forked tongue and yellow razor-sharp teeth, exhaling dark fumes from his now flattened nostrils.

That was how the demons killed you for the umpteenth time.

~

Forgive me, my dearest. I could not save you. It would mean nothing if I counted how many deaths you have been through. If I had torn the spirit barrier to reach you, a storm would have buried this town. But this is what I can do: I will remind you of what you are and what we mean to each other.

We are a soul; a cosmic pair, an eternal couple, an infinite dyad. You are my mortal being. I am your other self, your chi, your angel, your guardian spirit, your dreaming eye. I absorb mortal knowledge as one-half of your mind. I see all your thoughts through good and ill from one lifeform to the next. You think and I hear, I speak and you hear, but the spirit barrier separates me from your physicality.

Wave after wave, souls emerge from the Creator's heart, the centre of all light. We exist to preserve the spirit barrier, the chasm between mortality and infinity, as there would be horrendous consequences if that rift is directly bridged. Hence, the significance of separating into mortals and spirits. Lifeform after lifeform, you live and die, and the barrier opens to reunite us briefly before drawing you back to mortality, into a new lifeform. We have walked the higher dimensions, expanding our knowledge, conceiving and terminating realities, inventing concepts, investigating constructs, and daring each other to take chances with the unknown.

As emissaries of the Abyss, the Devourer of Worlds—the Bottomless Pit, where even the Creator has no power—the demons hunt us for our light until we have nothing left to birth new life forms. This is Transcendence, and what follows it is the slow degradation into mindless minions with no will except to feed the Abyss, dark shadows eager to possess mortal bodies and hunt the light of souls.

The Deed, a host of rebellious souls known for fighting against Transcendence, has been on the run for ages, leaving one rumour after another of a last stand against the Order. I have heard spirits whispering about the Deed meeting somewhere on Earth, that they have raised a construct to unbind souls marked for Transcendence—something about a portal to another universe, where the Abyss has no power.

"It might be true," said the first spirit, who was also marked for Transcendence. "I should have joined them long ago. They are so brave, doing all that despite the Infinite Laws. Sometimes I wonder why souls cannot share their light with those who have lost theirs."

The other spirits, less concerned about anything involving the Deed, told the first one, "You should be trying to feel your mortal one last time, like our sibling over there." They looked at me, nodding encouragingly. Before I could force a smile in response, they all drifted to where I stood between two iroko trees, watching your corpse. From the way they crossed whole neighbourhoods with their few strides, I could tell they were younger spirits, born in the Seventh Wave. One of them placed a hand on my right shoulder and asked, "How long do you have until you transcend?"

"Two Earth days," I answered.

"How many lives have you had on Earth?"

"Nine."

"Could you tell us about them?" the third spirit asked, having a glow of curiosity I, too, once had.

I smiled easily and told them just as I tell you now.

THE GOOD SPIRITS

~

Would you have had an easier life as Loveday Okoro if you had remembered your past lives? Perhaps memories of past lives would give mortals complete clarity to the essence of being. That Sunday morning, you did not just imagine life as a Catholic missionary. It was almost an exact memory of your seventh life in this world. During your first tour of what would later become the island state of Bogo, in the Bight of Bonny, you were shown a shorter route to the main town from the chapel.

"This clearing was once a sacred ground," the village chief said. He pointed to a spot with scented fern and beanstalks. "My great-great-grandfather and his companions, when they discovered this island, prayed to the good spirits right here."

"Oh," you nodded. "Then why do you let foreigners use it?" You were eager to hear him affirm the mysterious ways of God.

"The spirits have taught us that good can come from anywhere," the translator interpreted. "You see, the good spirits are everywhere. They guide us through every age. We see as they see. We will tell you to leave if that is their instruction. We have the village square now for prayers and offerings. This clearing is our gift to foreigners so they, too, can be close to the good spirits."

They believe in angels, you wrote in your journal later that evening—the same journal that became a theology classic after decades of being scrutinised by the Vatican. *The people of Bogo believe in angels, which they call the good spirits. Doesn't this confirm Father Ernest's belief that angels have been visiting peoples of Africa long before the arrival of the first missionaries? How ironic it is that 'dark' is the term used to describe a continent with so much light, with so many mysteries to reveal. I tell you, brethren, the revealing sight of God, He who sees all, is cast upon the land.*

~

Do you recall your life as a pirate, and how you stole a monarch's ship to help free hundreds of Africans bound for the Americas? Or your life as the Leopard King of Great Nubia, whose lover was a Persian sorcerer? Or your days as a lecturer who turned his house into a home for underprivileged children impacted by the Nigerian-Biafran War? Or that time, in your fifth life here, when I spent so much light trying to pull you out of the Mississippi? In the water, you looked like a sunken treasure chest lost not because of a storm or a battle at sea, but because it was too heavy for a vessel to hold.

Now you lie in this casket, unable to live again.

~

Your father was here earlier to identify the corpse before tomorrow's funeral. He left the casket lid open, pleading a favour with the mortuary attendant to keep the lights on, explaining that this would be all the light you could get before the funeral and that he thought you needed it. For someone who believes the dead know nothing and have no thoughts, he must think less of that now that it is you who has died. He touched your right cheek and I wanted to scream another nightmare at him for ignoring the tenderness he should have regarded when you were alive, but I am grateful that his chi made him consider our need for light at this final hour.

He was holding a fragrant sunflower and I almost cried as he fixed it in your hair, just above your forehead. When did he see the significance of that girly—as he called it—photograph of you, to know that you would have loved to be buried with flowers? Maybe he has seen and read the journal you hid in your bookshelf.

I cannot tell what this perfume is but it is familiar, and it is not from the flower in your hair. It smells like scented dew on freshly trimmed grass. I hear spirits whispering into the night wind. They are speaking in unison, so

I know they are talking to me. I want to believe what they are saying but I doubt that we can still be saved. Another mortuary attendant has arrived for their midnight shift. Your father's favour ended with the previous shift, so this one will shut the casket and turn off the lights.

~

The attendant just shut the casket but I still smell it. That fragrance, like scented dew on freshly trimmed grass. Our last light is shrinking but I am overwhelmed by this possibility of salvation. Then all of the past and all things erased wrap around your sentience. The darkness grips the dot of light; I see through the darkness and it sees through me; its void of a mouth drawing you in right to your last name in your last life. But just as the Abyss is about to touch me, the dot of light explodes as an avian-shaped spark. We are now a bright star rising from the void. This must be the portal to the other universe. This must be the way to our new existence.

Omnipresent

ROSELINE MGBODICHIMMA

Night has come. The room is dark and closing unto itself. Odogwu has summoned us as usual. His voice reverberates as he calls out to us, echoes accompany his baritone. When Odogwu sits down on his stool, his body splatters on the floor. He is made like a mat, so he folds and coils back into himself from time to time. He is feared. Everybody dreads him, except me. Our meeting is supposed to be a sent forth. The brother spirits had chosen a household for everyone and we knew which womb we were going to come from and when we were expected to leave. But I was going to be different.

~

The first mother I came through tried to save me by mutilating my body. She took rusted metal, heated it in a fire, and melted it into my skin, but I still left. She did not understand that our kind was elite. No human had the luxury of experiencing us twice. She had three daughters before me and they left five years later. Her prayers are frail and her chi is weak or how else did she keep getting children like us? Half human and heavy spirit. I left her by falling from a pepper tree, a flimsy way to leave.

~

After I left, I told Odogwu I will now re-enter the world on my own terms. I no longer wanted to be mutilated by human beings in the name of love.

They wanted to keep me as theirs, to watch me become. But spirits do not understand becoming.

Nobody dared to question Odogwu's allotment, but I did and it angered the brother spirits. How could a woman spirit like me choose where to go and when to leave?

The last time a woman spirit fought to have her way, the spirits made her life a living hell. They inflicted her with diseases till she was too sickly to roam the earth and she begged to return. Nobody wants to go to earth and not enjoy life. She now sits silently during meetings and has refused to be human again, not even after Odogwu promised her a rich family and thirty years of luxury on earth. I pity her because she is missing out.

~

Humans like to feel, feast and love. I want it too. We all want it. But we must always come back to Odogwu because we can not deny who we are in the spirit, even if we wanted to. We are a limbless and mindless lot. Our race is a spiritual thing and the only glory we have is that we are able to navigate two worlds. Many of us are heartless. Many of us are loveable. I am a mix of both. Nothing grows out of us except in human form, not breasts, not limbs, not nostrils. We exist as water and we communicate like the closing of a cave.

~

I told Odogwu I had found where I wanted to go and the uproar was too much. The brother spirits were roaming in anger. Why Odogwu favours me more than others, I don't know.

"Why Chief?" Odogwu asks me.

"I like one of his wives," I said. I had been monitoring her for months. She was peaceful and stoic.

"I want to be reborn through her" was all I said and Odogwu put me in Asa's womb.

Before he could utter another word, Nkume, a brother spirit started shouting. I knew not every spirit liked my guts, but Nkume's own was deep hatred. I understood why he was bitter. He was born to a king and was supposed to rule. But he was summoned back by the spirits on the day of his coronation. There is no spirit that does not want to rule a part of the earth. Nkume's departure was shameful, he did not even have the luxury of a ceremonious exit. Other spirits like him died in battles or fell from trees. But he slipped on the bathroom floor and hit his ears on the iron pail. When the time came for him to parade himself to the people as their soon-to-be king, he was nowhere, minutes later he was found lying naked and stone-cold on the bathroom floor. His parents were devastated but human beings must move on from hurt except they are trying to die, as for we that have swallowed death, we sit with it, the more the pain marinates, the deeper we understand how far beyond our form is. Rumor has it that Nkume tried to dive back into his body. They said he ran to the bush and hovered on a palm tree for days before he was dragged back into our realm. Nkume's departure was not the arrangement he had with Odogwu, but Odogwu's ways are not our ways. Nobody questions a man of the spirit. He formed this world and gave us a community, some of us had been roaming on trees for ages. We needed a place to rest, we wanted many more chances to experience the world and Odogwu gave us that chance. He does not answer to anyone, except some high spirits and they are unknown.

~

"You will go and you will come back when you like, but do not overstay or else..." Odogwu said to me. Odogwu left the remaining words unsaid.

Odogwu had given me freedom and washed his hands off the repercussions in between. I was mute because it was one thing to be human and another thing to be human without the full backing of Odogwu, it was similar to being a naked madman parading the roads to the jest of street children. But you see me and risk, five and six.

Odogwu was kind to me and only summoned me when I was in the bush or when I was chopping wood early in the morning. Nobody in my new home knew I was answering to a higher power with foam coming out of my mouth and my legs jerking uncontrollably. It was my secret. My spirit left and came back fast and furious. My Mother, Asa, was sensitive. That woman knew I was not ordinary and she chose to respect it by not asking questions. It is what I have always wanted, a human who understood it was best not to unravel spiritual things.

~

In our realm, everyone was free to express their anger. If you needed revenge you met Odogwu and he enabled it. If you are victorious after a hit, then you are a victor. If you are not, you are not. The brother spirits knew I wanted Chief because I wanted a large family. I wanted a bond with people with whom I shared the same womb. I wanted to be part of humanity again, to not be spirit forever. But things started to fall apart.

Abasi, my brother, suddenly died, and I suspected foul play. I had just bathed him and my mother fed him. He was not sick. He was not one of us. Next thing, his chest was swelling and almost reaching the ceiling and his breathing pattern reminded me of our spirit chant. I ignored it because bad things happen to human beings, even without the influence of bad spirits. It could have been a coincidence. I showed my mother where to bury him. We were still mourning him when Ani left, it was nothing like I had seen before. He was playing football with the other children and they brought him back with his knees squeezed together like a plastic bottle. His hands did the same thing, they were clasped together in a permanent akimbo and nobody could separate them. Chief had called a doctor, the best in the whole village. Ani screamed as they tried to untangle him from himself. The doctor was confused, he was untangling Ani like a rope. Ani came down with a high fever after the untangling and he died. Ezenwa and Ike also died in a strange way.

I blame Odogwu. Odogwu told me with his body language to stay as long as I desired but I should not overstay. He did not tell me this was the punishment. I wanted to experience childbirth and die when my offspring is strong enough to navigate life. I wanted the fruits of my human womb to create a family tree that continued to bear fruit even after I am gone. Is that one overstaying?

How could Odogwu let Nkume and the brother spirits punish me like this. As if taking my brothers was not enough he let death meet my mother. I had done everything I could and still, my mother was not moving. More people were pouring in and crying. I moved out and I went to my brother's grave.

~

Ezenwa and Ike were twins, the most beautiful and bubbly creatures I had met in my human life. I know you will think it is absurd but they both died from laughter. We gathered with our mats, to listen to the wives take their turns in telling the children moonlight stories. One wife spoke of the tortoise and how it was a trickster, we all giggled as she spoke. She was a fantastic storyteller. She would squat and stump her feet slowly to describe how the crab crawled out of his shell. She opened her two eyes wide and adjusted her wrapper to describe how greedy the tortoise was. She jumped and landed on the sand to show us how the tortoise broke its shell. It was epic, and even though I hated her, I began to laugh like others. Long after we were done laughing, Ezenwa and Ike's laughter lingered, they could not stop laughing. They rolled and laughed till their lips refused to bounce back together, their ribs became visible from their sides and their teeth quivered. I wish I was playing, but they laughed their way into breathlessness. It was on this day that all the wives concluded that my mother was a witch. It was also the day that I remembered Nkume and his thunderous laughter like poison, the ones that never stopped until Odogwu commanded it so. How could Nkume possess two innocent boys with his deadly laughter.

~

I was ready to let the death of my brother's slide because a woman is a passage and my mother's road was still very fertile, more paths could still come out of her as long as my father continued to climb her and he loved to climb. So I don't understand why she is no longer breathing?

~

For the first time, I prayed to the God the humans say died on the cross, let Him come and see what has happened. I am sure he did not answer me because he likes to mind his business. Did I call Him when I struck the deal with Odogwu? Why then will he respond to me now?

Nkume has touched my mother's life and he must remove his hand from it before they lower her into the grave. I am screaming now and my head is spinning. Everyone has gathered to hold me because they have never seen me like this. Me that wears pain like a mask, me that gulps agony, it is this same me that is crying my first human cry.

I will return to our realm today. I will get revenge on the brother spirits, but I will start with Nkume. First, I need to find the body he is using to operate. If you have mind, follow me.

LOVE GROWS STRONGER IN DEATH

Across Vistas

MIRACLE ELVIS IFESINACHI

The length of the road doesn't surprise me. It never did and it won't start now. Distance has always been something you consider ecstatic so you stretch everything; feed it with time, spread out every one of its edges, and linger on every step.

This expanse where I wheel you along seems endless. It is a good thing that wheelchairs don't run on gas. So, we can go on and on. Maybe I'm your gas. That's why when I feel almost empty—when my legs start to quiver from my ankles, and my eyes start closing from how weary they have become—I stop and look into those eyes of yours. I need that reminder that they can still watch, still steady me.

The hospital has now become a speck in the distance and ahead of us, the lawn runs yonder, and because our circumference is bounded by the horizons, it feels like we are gaining ground as we move—plundering earth-space from the sky.

Yesterday I asked you what it is about destinations that bore you. What's the joy if things don't have an end? What is the beauty of the day if all the noise, excitement, and motion don't wound up into the calm of the night? You didn't respond. You cannot, because age has rounded up your voice to a destination a few months back. It did for your legs too, but I know these eyes of yours. I have studied them since I was a child. I have watched them fall on people and then hold a stare. And like pouring salt on earthworms, these people would first wriggle animatedly, then appear puzzled, before transitioning to looking exhausted. Everyone left your presence a flailing mass of themselves, and even then, your eyes would look dissatisfied—the want will still be fresh and unending. Unlike with others, these eyes have made me strong, and over the course of my life, they have buoyed me. They still do.

You want to take a piss, and you eye the tall grass to the left. I gently assist you out of the wheelchair and guide you towards the grass. This has become my daily routine for the past week: I enter your room in this new home of yours, wheel you out into the distance, and bring you back inside when my phone rings with the doctor's voice on the other end, "Mrs. Oluchi, it's time for your grandmother's evening session."

I'm aware of your disdain for Doctor Kwesi. You hate how he meticulously allocates time for every detail. It frustrates you when he sends student nurses to your room to boss you around in the guise of finely chosen healthcare registers. "It's time to get up, Grandma Chinyere," one of them would say while another insists, "Please use your tea to swallow your drugs." Despite the seemingly polite nature of these requests, you know that they are thinly veiled commands. True requests allow for the freedom to comply or not. But whether you like it or not, you must wake up at 8 am and you must line up for morning sunlight—with all these other men and women who, like yourself, could barely get off their beds without help—on mats that made your back itch afterwards. By 9:20 am, you must force down the slimy oatmeal and bland pancakes that taste like stale, dried-out fish, and wash it all down with a mug of lukewarm tea. At 10 am, you take the first round of pills, followed by a 30-minute rest you never seem to want. But when I arrive with the wheelchair, your face brightens, ready for a change of pace.

You keep longing for this distance. Last week, when I visited and had finished helping scratch your back—a task that always precedes transferring you to the wheelchair—you asked me why you needed a 30-minute rest. You wondered if anyone needed to rest after lying down for so long. You asked what the pills were for. What ailment they were supposed to cure. You would squawk and wriggle a finger or your toes when I hit the spot that itches the most while scratching your back. I like the face you make when this happens, so I would linger on the spot until your eyes dance, your nerves surrendering to a tickle. I still don't know the last time you laughed. Did that end too, your laughter? As I rode you out of the building that day, I told you that the drugs were not curing anything, but that you could consider them friends. That you were up against the door that symbolized the end of your life and you were pushing hard to keep it shut, and that these pills helped push along with you.

We have found a spot. I help you sit on your ankles and I draw down your pants. I wonder if your obsession for elongation happened in lovemaking too. How long did it take you to climax? I wonder what you think of sex; its brevity and sometimes, perfunctoriness. Did you stop having sex disappointed by its fleetingness, or did you have it so often, hoping that somehow someday you were going to be able to stretch pleasure, to fill desire itself with time?

You've asked me so many questions since I first visited two weeks ago. Why was I so thin? Why did I cut my hair short? I said I wasn't thin. I said that I would always look thin to you for as long as you weren't cooking my meals anymore. And I cut my hair into a style. I gave the sides a fade, I wanted a new look. Your hair is spongy and the strands all have a conspicuous inequality in their length. The ones crowning your forehead have gone scanty, a few strands missing and a few others short—too short to join the rest at the back to form that spongy tuft when your hair is packed and held with a hair band. But everyone would know you used to have long hair. And because when I stroke it, your eyes dance, I know you cared about it. Lately, your questions have been more difficult, like when you asked about Jude.

I walked you through details I knew you already knew. Maybe it was just to remind you of these things, or maybe it was my way of re-representing the facts and reaffirming to myself that I wasn't wrong. That I tried, even though I may not have done everything the best way, and that based on the things I knew and was exposed to about marriage, no one would consider me a failure in it.

We return to the wheelchair. I have had an ample look at your eyes, perhaps your whole being. I take my position behind you, my hands firm on the chair's push handles. I confirm that you are well reclined, and that your neck sits well on the push axis. I am well-recharged to take another mile.

The wheels are on again. I see the little shake of your head as we go faster, and I know that you secretly enjoy the rush. How the caster wheel mows grasses along our path, in sync with the rear wheel that collects the fallen grasses and clamps them into thin lines, such that we seem to be trailed by braided cornrows of grasses. On this flight, I'm finding these past years without you forming into strips, as though somewhere along the line, a montage slid across my vision.

The first day I met Jude was at Aunty Nneka's wedding. He had been ridiculously cliché: like most Best Men, he was dressed in the same blue silk shirt tucked into black trousers, same bow tie, same trendy men's haircut, and held the same effusive smile and a gaze of uncertainty. He seemed nervous too. So nervous that I wondered how he was going to hold up with his Best Man speech. The speech was equally cliché, even his tears too. Someone that typical was never supposed to pique anyone's attention. And he didn't mine, particularly, but after Aunty Nneka introduced us—me in my chief bridesmaid uniform and him in his very quintessential Nigerian best man outfit—and after he joked about best men and chief bridesmaids always going out together, I started to fear that for a person that stock-charactered, one could perhaps tell the day he was going to die. So, I proceeded to search for something that would remotely appear unexpected—a modicum of unconventionality in him. It was this search that made me ask for his number. That made me go out with him on two occasions. Then because on the second date, he made a joke about ordering Eba and Egusi on dates, I decided I would have sex with him. I had certified him typical and thought that the way he would make love would most likely be God's designed manner of lovemaking.

If God isn't a woman, then he must be sworn to chivalry if he indeed designed lovemaking the way I and Jude made it. Jude had waited for me to toggle at the straps of my bra before he made to take them off. He let me take off my underwear by myself and only started to undress after I had ripped off two buttons on his shirt and broken the zipper of his trousers. He was gentle, and although he gasped lightly at intervals, the expression on his face was as though thrusting into me was seamless—too seamless it bothered me a little. But when he would ejaculate, he held on to me so tight, and groaned so loud that I stifled laughter. Like sex, everything with Jude would continue that way: the way he could seem indifferent in one moment and resolve into a yearning in the next. The way he could be so mature then while away in petulance.

I stop the wheels now and turn to see how far we have come, or gone. Our trail is beautiful. The cornrows patterned grasses just run on and on, in zig-zags and straight lines and curves and zig-zags again, I want to take a picture. I turn you around to take a look. I watched as you gasped. Your face lightens. It is the sort of thing you like. More so, we can't find the beginning. Somehow, it seems blurred into the backdrop of the hospital buildings. My phone rings and the light in your face dies. You know it's Dr Kwesi. You raise a hand, making to touch me. It is slow but in a way that shows you had intended to hurry. I know you don't want me to take the call. I know you hate Doctor Kwesi because, first, he is a part of the Home; also because he has become the one whose words you have to live by. And his words, they bring destinations. Your eyes won't stop stressing how he gives time to everything, and recently, they—your eyes—have started to beckon on me to join you in hating him. They say, *how dare he give time to your life? How dare he say you have cancer and won't see Christmas?* Christmas is in two days and I know you can't wait to look him in the face and scream liar! To tell him that this whole prison life called palliative care is a waste of your time. I want to see those lights in your eyes again, so I turn off my phone, turn you around and we journey on.

Our wedding was at St Nicholas and the vicar was the same priest who wedded Aunty Nneka and her husband. Even though he kept telling us that he perceived the chemistry between us from Aunty Nneka's wedding; even though he said that he knew we would end up together; and even though he said he felt fulfilled after wedding us both, I couldn't stop thinking about how it had been just 5 years since Aunty Nneka's wedding and they were already divorced. But I never really liked Nduka, Aunty Nneka's husband. I disliked how too-remotely-Igbo he was, starting every line with *Nna men* or *Odi egwu* as though everything surprised him. I hated the way his stomach had grown into a larger pot than the last time I saw him, and how he seemed to pride himself in it, rubbing it with his hands all the time amidst laughter. He was an importer; wines from Italy, cars from Germany, and something else from China. But he was also just forty and didn't need to always show himself off as a pot-bellied nouveau riche Igbo importer. So, when six months before my wedding, my mother called to tell me that Aunty Nneka was getting a divorce, and that Nduka had been hitting her, I had first imagined his hands tied to the ceiling, me puncturing his big stomach with a needle.

In the years to come, I would try to imagine Jude hitting me. Sometimes it seemed I wanted him to. I wanted to see what it would look like for him to go all red with his veins daring to bust out of his skin, then him throwing me against the wall or grabbing my hair and hitting me until I bled. But he would never. There were things he never could do. He lived constantly with an apologetic grace around him, as though he had somehow offended the world so much that it would take him a lifetime to redeem himself. But this grace looked so beautiful on him that you would rather respect him than pity him—you would consider him a graceful man rather than an honest repentant.

He asked me about everything. Most times they felt like seeking permissions. Simple permissions. Like when he says, *Honey, I need to tell my boss we need more printers. These minor things are integral to business growth.* A vein would appear on his head signalling that he had peaked in stress. And when I said *yes, you need to*, the vein disappeared, and his face would return to calm as though by me saying yes, he could now tell his boss and his boss would do as expected and the business would bring expected returns. Other times they felt like he honestly didn't know. Jude was an accountant. He worked for a bank with whom I was already an account holder before I met him at all, and Jude had people run up and down answering *Yes, sir! Sorry, sir! Okay, sir!* to mere blinks of his eyes. So, when those other times he would say, *honey do you think it would rain tonight?* And because of the way he would look at me with childlike inquisitiveness, I would look out of the window and gaze at the sky. And when I responded in the affirmative, I would commence a prayer inside me that it actually rained. Most men said, *Queen. My Queen.* Maybe Jude did too, many times, but constantly, I felt like a goddess—omnipotent. You know Grandma, how as a child I was obsessed with redefining the world. How I wrote a petition to the school management when my class teacher chose a boy to be the class captain over me. How I staged many protests at the University and was threatened with expulsion several times. Grandma, I had an opinion of how the world should be and was hell-bent on seeing it come to fruition. It was a fight I perhaps got addicted to, and so Jude coming into my life and letting me run it the way I did, put me in a position my feisty younger self could have thought lofty. But I must admit it was more than my mind could harbour. So, it rendered my anger, my vigour, and my grit unnecessary. What was their use when all they boiled for and even much more was already presented at my feet? As seamlessly as how he sometimes brought breakfasts in trays with a glass full of cranberry juice while I was still in bed.

Across from where we are now, I can see people in tiny specs, such that if it were to be an artwork, a tiny stroke of black would do for one human. There are small houses too, we may just be about to enter a village. From the way your eyes are fixated on that part of the distance, I know you can see them too. I stop the wheels, reach into one of the pockets, and withdraw a bottle of water. I let you have some. Much of your portion runs down your jaw through to your abdominal, wetting its path along. When it circles in between your laps and the wet patch rises vibrantly on that part of your hospital gown, I watch your eyes. They seem to laugh. I join in the laughter.

The laughter goes on until I decide it is time I ask my questions. *Is your perception of people eternal, Grandma? Would you never find amusing later the one you first found repulsive? Do you love on and on and hate likewise?*

I engage the caster wheels, and we are creating patterns again. This time it is across the top of what now seems like a hill because the sight in front of us is a village within a valley. I briefly think of picking you up and raising you above my head, supporting you only with my hands. I will have you caught against the sky, facing down towards the villagers like Simba from *The Lion King*. I whisper this into your ears as we go, I even hum the 'Awimbawe Awimbawe' song, but you don't even smile. You clearly have forgotten *The Lion King*. Or you just don't want to answer my question.

~

I told Jude I was pregnant on a Christmas Eve. We had spent the day at a supermarket two streets away from our estate, stocking up every space in the car with Christmassy items. I chose most of the things. Maybe everything except the small neon ball that releases a spectrum of colourful lights and bell sounds when hit against a surface. I had urged him to take something, and he had skimmed through the store before reaching for the neon ball. He had this boyish smile as he cradled the thing in his palms. He knew I was saying *'Really?'* so he kept his head down. I liked it when he seemed shy. Because he was always the one caring and trying to say and do the right things—by right things, I mean things that made me happy. His shy state gave me a sense of authority, but not as one who demanded that things be done for them, rather as one who did for people. His shyness allowed me to care for him. But that day, beyond the fact that I enjoyed him being shy, I took his choosing a ball, a typical child's toy, as his subtle way of communicating his readiness for a child. It had been 4 years since we got married.

Dr Nkechi and I had previously considered several ways I could creatively break it to Jude that I was pregnant. Because I had visited Dr Nkechi so frequently in the past three years in search of a solution to my barrenness, and because one of the first three sentences I made to her was, Please, *I don't want my husband to know about this*, she had become more than just my gynaecologist. And although she kept saying, *You look perfectly fine, Oluchi. You should bring in your husband for us to check him too,* she still didn't say a word to him, even though the hospital was just opposite Jude's bank. That's how much of a friend and confidant she became.

I suggested that I surprise him in his office. I would have his colleagues join me in my little game. Dr Nkechi suggested something less ostentatious, something about telling him at breakfast. Later, perhaps because we couldn't come up with something satisfying enough, I reminded myself how typical a man my husband was. He wouldn't even notice the brilliance or mediocrity in the means.

So, on the ride home after shopping, I raised my dress up above my tummy and asked if he noticed anything. He smiled and said amid a mild laughter, "You now eat too much."

"Yeah. Maybe that's because we have become two eating all the food."

His eyebrows furrowed—this was how his body signalled excitement, desire, and surprise. "What do you mean?"

His eyes were still on the road, but since his hands seemed to be flailing—as though his body was somehow losing all its energy, starting from his hands—I asked that he pull over.

Mama, Jude seemed like a quenching bulb. You know how when there is an irregular supply of power, how the fluorescent may appear robust and larger from the excess outlet of voltage and suddenly seem shrunken from how the light dies out slowly. That was how Jude's face looked. His vibrantly yellow skin appeared to darken immediately after he said, "You're pregnant, darling?"

Whilst my mind joggled between the options of this being excessive joy or crass disappointment, I feared he was going to fall sick. And he did. Jude puked for almost five minutes. I had to drive him to Dr Nkechi.

In an expanse like this Mama, there should be wild animals. Maybe not wild per se, but not domestic either. Like squirrels and monkeys. But we have walked for hours now and we have not seen anything that you would not see on a regular Lagos street. Besides, why would they situate the Home here? Somewhere almost nameless, far removed from richly inhabited areas—from people. Why would they situate a home meant to give quality to a lifetime that's supposedly wrapping up in a place this ostracised, deprived of the rising and falling conspicuousness of living and life?

I see that your head is moving in earnest, I am making the same points you've been making. Who knows, we are far away already. I could escape with you.

~

Oh, you don't like the idea? Why? You hate this place.

You don't want me to commit any more crimes?

This is not incriminating. This is going to be for me, redemption. Giving you a great end could be my redemption—my catching up with a hand that has long beckoned on me to pull me upwards, out of this well of regrets, shame, sadness...

You hate that I say end?

Mama, how do you still believe this illusion of immortalizing things? Of evading the fate of dying? Mama, you have lived well so far, and I'd recommend you accept death with open arms. You never can tell what you may do next, what inherent damage you could cause this world. Please leave with the much applause and boos alike that you have been able to garner. I am talking about you Mama, not Jude. I have come to heal, not to open healing wounds.

You slide your hand into my hand. *Where is he now,* you ask?

Mama, I loved Jude. I want you to know this. I come around and kneel in front of you. You lean my body forward onto you so that my face is on your breast. I am crying, I want you to understand that I loved Jude. I want you to save me from doubting that fact myself.

I engage the wheels again.

Jude had been using drugs; drugs that reduced his sperm count. He never wanted a child. I watched him sit beside me on the bed I was lying on. His face seemed old as he pleaded. Not old as in advanced in years, but old as in stale. Like a half-sliced orange that has been sucked off its juice and left to be fed upon by microbes. He was pleading tearfully. This was a different Jude. Jude who never even looked like he wanted anything, who was always empty of desperation. I said nothing to him. Mama, you should know: you know that feeling when one's larynx appears broken, or worst, tampered with, such that now, it seems every organ in one's body is speaking—sharing one another's plight, thus one's aloof facial expression is the mask, the facade to an anthropotomy in chaos.

I wouldn't speak to him for days. Even on the days when I went to see Dr Nkechi, and sat there for hours having her joggle through all the encouraging words she got, weeping in response at intervals. I would return to bed and remain in it till the following day when even the very scent of Jude's perfume was no longer in the air of our bedroom.

But Mama, it was the first time Jude asked me anything that seemed to matter. If he had piled up all the favours he had won from the ones he had offered me in our time as spouses—as in the game of quid pro quo—then asking this one favour may not seem too much. Maybe nothing in fact. Maybe this is what I considered. Maybe I also considered the fact that this was my 'what do you give a man who has everything' moment; better phrased, 'what do you give a man who wants nothing but one thing.' You give him that one thing. The one thing could be everything. That is what I have grown to know love to be—sacrifice, compromise, commitment... Mama, you should know: beyond the butterflies and canoodling, the very crux of love is 'compromise'. It is this that yokes two together.

So, I went to Dr Nkechi on the evening of the Monday that would make the foetus three weeks old, at about the time Jude would be rounding off at work. I hoped that I would catch a glimpse of him walking out of the bank into his car whilst the operation to remove our child was being done. I hoped that he would see how much of myself I was giving to him. Also, that somewhere lodged within his lowly, yet firm, frame I would find him worthy of it.

But the child would not die. She would not allow herself to be pulverized or turned to blood in her own mother's womb. I don't know what about life she saw that made her hang on to it so tightly. Why would she even want a mother who was pushing her as far back as to death? Why!

On the morning I delivered the baby, Jude was the first face I saw. He was standing with a bouquet with a small smile on his face. He and Dr Nkechi had taken the previous night shopping for baby clothes. On the drive home, he looked at me from the rear-view mirror and nodded slightly before saying. "Nkem, Dr Nkechi told me you tried. Thank you. But after seeing the baby, I'm grateful it didn't work."

Mama, I have cried many times in my life. But I had never felt myself drowning in my own tears. It was as if there was so much fluid inside me, too much to be let out through just my eyes and nose, so I felt my heart swelling. Jude was silent, and even though he didn't make choking sounds like I did, his eyes and nose ran too. And at some point, when the blur in my eyes had waned off enough for me to hold gazes with him in the rearview, I heard him say softly, in a tone softer than whispers, almost like thoughts, "We have done everything together, Nkem. Even crying. Let's raise her together."

You want to know when things changed. I know. But it's important you know we had all the moments. We felt all the butterflies. We loved each other and the baby. Jude asked that we name her after me. Oluchi. She indeed had my resemblance.

Oluchi had a bright yellow complexion. Dr Nkechi asked that we name her Apunanwu—untainted by the sun—but however mystical the name sounded, I would not give my daughter a generic name. But Oluchi was indeed bright, almost to the point of shining. She was smallish, but you could tell that she was going to be tall, and that her hair was going to be dense and long, and that her eyes were going to be a little outsized for her face yet perfect. You could as well see the full-frame adult in her. Dr Nkechi said it was me, that I had now gotten a new pair of eyes. The sort of eyes that gave the vision of a mother. I would wonder if it was the same eyes that made me see everyone that I cared about in her too. Jude, myself, my late parents, you, Mama, and sometimes, however vaguely, Dr Nkechi herself. But it was as if she bettered all these qualities. Like how her complexion was a pro version of Jude's. Like her whole being was saying, "Y'all think you nailed it? Watch me!"

I see a crab along our paths. I always thought they were only found around water. This has been a long ride on sand and through vegetation. Who knows, we could just be approaching a beach.

You ask me why I didn't ever bring Oluchi to you. There was no time, Mama.

You say you had time, what exhausted mine? Time isn't always the same thing as being alive, Mama.

You are angry. You say I know you would have cared for her like you raised me. Well, Mama, you don't care for a dead child. You don't raise a dead child. All the yellow in her complexion is meaningless if her heart is cold and dark and dead.

Oluchi died on her 30th day on Earth. I was returning from the kitchen with a jar of something and a glass cup when I saw the bloodbath in our bed. The jar and the glass dropped. I rushed to my child. Her eyes bled; her nose bled. And some other places I couldn't tell because all I saw was my Oluchi in a pool of blood. It was fast. Jude walked out of the bathroom; his hands still had blood. "Darling, I wanted her to bear your name to see if it was going to help me. To see if naming her after the most precious thing in the world to me would help me stand her."

Jude was still talking and the echo of the clattering glass still rang when I found myself driving his head through every glass and against every surface. He felt too light for his manly frame. Hahaha. I thought he died too easily for a murderer. Hahaha. Maybe he wasn't a murderer after all. Hahaha. Maybe he wasn't in the way I am not. Hahaha.

~

I cannot make out what your eyes are saying this time. The batting, the dilations, the darting of your disappearing eyeballs. Every sign eludes me. Are you yelling at me, Mama? Is this hate you are communicating? Stop it, Mama. In the end, I hurt myself. They are all gone to obscurity where there is no hurt or heartbreak or the sheer uncertainties preinstalled in this life, nothing at all. I am the one here, Mama. I am here broken and deranged.

Oh, you aren't yelling? You're crying. Are these tears, Mama? You understand me. You do.

Mama, what did you do with grief? Did you try stretching it too? Did you desire its permanence?

You want me to sit.

I come around and sit some feet away from you. There's a small tingling in my back, so I lie on the ground and stretch my limbs. The ground seems soft but firm, as though if one falls from some height, you could hear a thud but the person wouldn't fracture any bone. My eyes catch the vast sky. I want you to see this too so I help you off the wheelchair, and we then lie by each other. Your eyes appear dilated and all the colours that have now appeared since I last saw you two decades ago—faded yellow, faded green, faded anything—seemed to dance. I know you want to be here till nightfall—you want to monitor the movement of the sun until it has disappeared from the sky. But we have to go back. There's food and water there—some of what you'll need to help your forlorn hope of immortality. All I have is a murderer's burden, all of it—the stigma, precisely.

You should go back, Mama. If for nothing else, I want you to go and look Dr Kwesi in the face when it's long past Christmas and say, "Asshole doctor, remind me today's date, please." I want you to have that one piece of sarcasm.

LOVE GROWS STRONGER IN DEATH

The Emails

THIRIKWA NYINGI

Talia sat at her desk staring out of the window with her laptop open in front of her. There had been a power blackout following a thunderstorm that lasted the whole afternoon and scared the wits out of the big grey tomcat that now rested on her lap. Now, the electrical appliances in the quiet house hummed and blinked with life after the power.

The distant rumble of thunder echoed through the trees. In the deepening twilight Talia's sombre face lay bathed in the soft light of the luminous laptop screen. Her hand toyed with the keys while she stroked the cat. The other hand put Talia's turbulent mind at rest.

She leant forward careful not to upset the cat and drew the curtains. Then she swept her hand over the glossy surface of her desk to brush away an imaginary speck. She noticed an unusual activity, so imperceptible she might have missed it had she not been expecting it. It was another email notification. She sat up and the movement awoke the cat. She set him on the floor and bent towards the laptop's screen as if unseeing and stared at the tiny icon of the new message.

Beads of perspiration glittered on her forehead as her fingers hovered over the keyboard. She hit a key. The email opened. *'Hi sweetie,'* it read, *'rained cats and dogs here. How is the weather down there? Remember to air the bedding tomorrow. Good nite dear.'* She felt giddy and a sudden constriction on her throat left her gasping for air.

Earlier, after much agitation of the mind, she had composed the two-worded email to her mother which simply read – hi mother – and waited with mounting dread for her mother's response. Her mind flew back to the previous evening when she feared the house was haunted.

The evening had been cool and quiet at first, a welcome relief from the blistering heat of the day. The furnace-like temperatures had rendered any form of useful activity pointless. By midday the house had become uninhabitable as the sun continued to burn. As she had walked outside to the cool shade of a nearby sycamore tree, a frightening noise sent her eyes scouring the cloudless sky for the source. She almost bolted back into the house in terror but checked herself at the last minute.

Perched at the top of one of the tall eucalyptus trees underneath which her mother's grave lay, was one of the ugliest and scariest bird she had ever seen. Its size alone was forbidding. It was swaying on a branch that looked like it could break off at any moment but even before the thought was out of her head a loud crack followed by a crashing noise, reverberated through the compound as the huge bird came tumbling down amid a wild flutter of wings and feathers before its fall was broken by the lower and heavier branches.

The screeching and cawing of the bird sent the smaller birds sheltering in the neighbouring trees. The big grey tomcat materialized from nowhere at a terrifying speed and darted past her frozen figure into the house. The bird flew down and landed on the gravestone before it thrashed its big wings in a cloud of dust and then flew away in ungainly manner.

A few minutes later after the cacophony had died down she walked down to her mother's grave which was now buried under broken twigs among other debris knocked down by the tumbling bird. She set to clearing it but before long she was overtaken by sleep and lay down next to the grave on a small patch of grass and dreamt that her mother had come up to her and said, "I have not been dead my daughter," she had then pointed at the grave and added, "that's someone else lying there." She had woken up in a cold sweat and disoriented before she found her bearings. The sun was by then a huge orange ball hanging low in the western horizon. She realized she had been crying in her sleep as the last rays of the sun cast long shadows across the compound.

She was still trying to come to terms with her mother's tragic death – almost a month later. Her life was snuffed out a short distance from their house by a juggernaut of a truck that appeared around the corner and rumbled down the street at full speed. She was hardly recognizable. She was rushed to the nearby government hospital by a good Samaritan but efforts to revive her by the doctors had been useless as she had lost a lot of blood.

The truck had disappeared around the bend without slowing down missing yet another pedestrian who jumped out of the way and fell headlong into a ditch filled with dirty water.

Darkness had settled upon the country and she moved off the graveside into the house when the idea of the emails hit upon her. Without wasting time she had fetched her laptop, opened it and typed '*Missing you badly dear mum*' and sent it to her late mother's address – not expecting any reply of course but only a feeble attempt at unburdening herself from the grief.

She was horror-stricken then when she got a reply almost instantly – *Missing you too dear. Sleep tight.* With trembling hands, she gripped the laptop with both hands and read the email again. Then she stared wide-eyed at the smiling profile picture of her mother and she felt goose bumps all over her body. "Can't be! Can't be!" she wailed in horror. She slammed shut the laptop and pushed herself away from the desk knocking over the chair in the process and scaring away the cat.

At the same time a sudden gust of wind banged shut the kitchen door causing her to jump. The cool and quiet evening transformed into a stormy night as the wind picked up. There was a great roaring noise outside the house as the trees lashed about in the wind.

Talia thought she heard a cracking sound outside the house but she had now become transfixed in the middle of her bedroom where she had fled in horror and was now staring at her mother's reflection in the mirror. There was another flickering of lights and the image in the mirror was gone.

It was the scariest night ever but she found herself in one piece when she woke up in the morning. She sat up in the bed upsetting the cat for the umpteenth time as she tried to recall the events of the night. And then it all came back in a flood. The emails! Of course, it was the emails! She almost went dizzy at this shocking realization. She swept back the blankets and swung her feet on the floor and gave her head some minutes to clear.

It took her some minutes to clear the passage to her bedroom where she had set furniture and other heavy stuff against the door to barricade herself from the malevolent spirit that could have been roaming outside. She tiptoed to her study hoping all the time that it had been a dream and peered round the doorway. Her barely touched supper was still at the desk as was the laptop next to it. She carried on for the rest of the day as if nothing untoward had taken place the previous night afraid to open the laptop and find evidence to the contrary.

At around noon the day turned dark as heavy rain clouds rolled across the sky enveloping the sun in their cushy folds. Talia's fresh-smelling laundry flapped from the long clothesline as it got blown by the sudden wind that smelled of wet earth. Fat raindrops were already hitting the parched ground by the time she got the laundry inside the house. For the next three hours or so she stood by the kitchen window enthralled as she watched the thunderstorm unleash itself.

Occasionally she would yelp in excitement as a deafening clap of thunder resounded all over the place until the ground shook making the dirty pile of utensils in the sink to rattle. The terrified cat had taken cover under the settee and every effort to entice it out in the open failed until the storm had passed. She had not realized there was a power outage until much later on when she tried on the television.

Sometime later when the power was back on she sat down at her desk and regarded the laptop with renewed interest and a sense of apprehension. Her mind was still troubled by the bizarre events of the previous night and she was averse to having a repeat.

It took her nearly an hour of pacing up and down the house before she reached the decision to take a peek at the laptop to confirm whether it had been a dream or not. She hesitated a bit and then clicked open the laptop and scrolled through the many emails in her inbox. She almost missed that particular one and she was at the point of sighing in relief when she checked the archived messages and there it was, tucked into a corner like a trapped mouse ready to spring away. She breathed in and out several times to compose herself and gather her wits and then she sent the briefest email she had ever sent that simply said, hi mum. And now her mother had responded – her dead mother. This thought perturbed her to no end. It was time she got to the bottom of it. However, since her mother was still responding to her emails from whichever netherworld she was she might as well continue the conversation with her, she figured.

And she fell to it with gusto of someone who had suddenly found her long-lost soul mate.

Hi mom, here it rained so hard Tabby disappeared under your favourite settee for hours she typed and smiled as she inserted a smiley face at the end of the sentence. Then a sad thought struck her and a sob escaped her. She missed her mother in a way she thought was not possible considering they were not even on talking terms at the time of her death.

They had had a quarrel over a man Talia was seeing and she had walked out of the house in a huff and rented a single room in town where she had been staying until her mother's death. It was three days later when she got a text message from her mother informing her she had gone away to visit a long-time friend in another part of the country and would stay for while – probably a month. 'Have a nice time dear' she had signed off. It was like they had never exchanged bitter words only three days before. She deleted the text in blind anger.

Her boyfriend broke up with her the next day after the quarrel with her mother. She blamed her mother for the break-up. It was some time later in the day when the call came informing her that her mother was in the hospital. Before she could even get a word out there was a beep or two before the line went dead. "Hello! Hello!" she shouted into the phone in desperation unable to make sense of anything but it was all in vain. The caller had hung up and was not even reachable. Her mother's phone too was dead. Frantic with worry she rode like one possessed on her mountain bike in the direction of the hospital where she learnt of her mother's death.

Ha Ha Ha! Oh poor Tabby! Hope now she is okay. Will be seeing you tomorrow. Gdnt. Her mother wrote. Talia could not understand what she meant about the last bit but she assumed her mother meant continuing the conversation the following day therefore she almost got a heart attack when she opened the door the following morning and saw her mother standing there with her bags wearing a broad smile.

She backed off into the house like she had seen a ghost. After she had recovered they learnt that a woman who had been reported missing was the dead woman. Talia felt a huge relief that her mother was back from the 'dead'

Ass Ears

CHOUROUQ NASRI

Fatiha is not the same person. Not since her mom died; not since she saw her new stepmom wearing her mom's jewellery only three months later. The pain is sharp, exquisite, unbearable. She knows by the way people stare at her that her face reveals the deep scars of a soul that had been bruised too many times. She viewed her life through the lens of numb detachment, seeing nothing but a blank, meaningless landscape. She waited to die, but she never did die.

Everything around her seemed different too, as if the whole world had become unfamiliar. Even the people she knew looked different. Her neighbours, her teachers, her classmates, her friends; Ammi Brahim, the grocery store owner; Ammi Hammad, the school guard. Everyone seemed like zombies with malevolent intentions towards her. There were even some people she didn't recognize at all. Sometimes, a neighbour would smile and wave to her as she trudged home from school, but she never smiled back. Instead, she would stare blankly at the ground.

It all started January 1st, 1965, the day her mother died while giving birth to Rahma, her youngest sister. Fatiha used to be filled with confidence and humour, all lit up and alive to the world. She was one of the brightest students at Lala Lyacoute Primary School for Girls, a special student whose cleverness, dedication, and genuine passion for learning called for all her teachers' admiration. She even won an award for the best composition in French the previous November. After her mother's death, the days and dates written on the blackboard and in her notebooks became meaningless. She felt weak and powerless, a bereaved child who could not be comforted. As a motherless girl, she struggled to battle her grief and stay on her feet. The world felt like a hollow shell, with nothing left to fill it but emptiness.

Fatiha is ten years old, but she seems to be already inching towards the end of childhood innocence. She was short when she joined the school at the beginning of the new session in September 1964. Now she is taller than most of her classmates. Every weekday, she walks to school through the garden that separates her apartment from Lala Lyacoute. The school is new, and the buildings are tall. They were built a few years after Morocco's independence and named after the late King Mohamed V's mother. Lala Lyacoute. The name has an elegant, royal cadence, to Fatiha's ears at least. The school's facade is green with undertones of grey. It contains a row of small, square windows high up to let in the daylight, and two doors—one at the far end of the building, for teachers, and a bigger one for students. Opposite the school lies the white balconies of the five-storey concrete building where Fatiha lives. From her room window, she can sometimes see children play in the huge courtyards behind the school's closed gates.

It is an unusually hot day in the middle of May. Fatiha is wearing a light summer dress with a sailor collar and white sandals that belong to her older sister, Naziha. Her hair is shiny black, straight, but dishevelled. The weight of the navy-blue school bag her mom had bought for her from lmdina back in September pulls her back as she pushes ploddingly towards Lala Lyacoute.

Fatiha is haggard and pale. Her skin is sallow, her eyes are ringed with fatigue, and her beauty has somewhat corroded. She looked like someone who barely got any sleep. Every night, as she tried to fall asleep, her mind would fill with memories of her mother, haunting her thoughts. She would lie awake for hours, finally drifting off for only a few hours at most, only to be jolted awake by the sound of her mother's voice echoing in her head. She would bury her head under the sheets and try to think of summer vacations in Bouchakour, where she could smell the scent of the earth and the scent of orange trees in the air. She could almost feel the warmth of the sun on her face. But these memories were too fragile, and they evaporated in seconds, leaving her mind swirling with other thoughts. Her mother's voice was louder now, like the hum of an aircraft overhead. She could not think of anything else, or even move a muscle, as her body felt heavy and stiff. She would feel exhausted in a way that made her feel disconnected from herself, as if she were floating in the air, a disembodied spirit looking down on a small, forlorn girl who was trapped in her own mind. All she wanted was to close her eyes and wake up in the morning to a world where her mother was still alive. She just wanted the clock to rewind itself to a time before she lost her mother. But of course, that was not possible. No matter how hard she wished, time could not turn back. She had to live in the present, a harsh reality where everything was different. The memories of her mother would never fade, but they would be tempered by the passing of time, like a river that had carved a channel through the landscape of her mind.

Fatiha arrives at school at 8:25 am, five minutes before classes were due to begin. Ammi Hammad, the school's cheerful, talkative guard is sitting in his chair by the school gate, nearly smothered in a woolly jellaba he wears despite the heat. He has olive skin and a pinched, long nose. He wears magnifying glasses that make his eyes look enormous. His silvery-brown hair, thinning at the crown but abundant elsewhere, looks as if it has not been brushed in a long time. Fatiha saw only a worn-out shell of a man, age weighing heavily on his features. He smiles when he sees her, exposing his big, discoloured teeth.

"Sbah lkhir abnti Fatiha, labass alik?"

Fatiha moves ahead without replying. Another dull day in Lala Lyacoute awaits her. She is not ready for it, and yet, she finds herself walking through the narrow colourfully tiled corridors that lead to the classroom, fumbling her way towards a grim life.

All students must line up in front of the classroom when they hear the first bell. They must wait for their teachers before entering their classrooms. The walls of Fatiha's classroom is painted yellow and red, with posters of birds and nature scenes. The closets are filled with dog-eared books, and two foldable blackboards stand at the front. Small windows, with white curtains, line the left side of the room.

Fatiha was in the fourth grade, and her Arabic class was taught by a new teacher named Ostada Zineb. Ostada Zineb was young, probably only 20 or 21 years old, and had only been teaching for a year or two. Ostada Zineb is beautiful, with bright green eyes and clear skin with the hint of a tan. She was previously in a relationship with Ostad Salah, who also works at the school. One day after a heated argument which happened in front of everyone, Ostada Zineb ended the relationship and got married to another man a few weeks later.

She used to be impeccably dressed, her long hair pinned back at the sides with bobby pins. But since her wedding, she discarded her short floral dresses and stylish little jackets and began to wear a black jellaba with a kob, and high heeled black shoes.

Since her return from her honeymoon, she has become uncharacteristically sour. There is something sly in her as she now seems to enjoy embarrassing students. She often tries to act cool by tossing a piece of chalk into the air and catching it, but she is often in a bad temper.

Whenever the closing bell rings, announcing the end of the classes, she often jumps from her seat, puts the chalk down, says the class is over, picks up her bag, and from the way she rushes off, half walking, half running, everyone can see how happy she is to escape from teaching and students.

This is not a class Fatiha looks forward to. She wishes she began her school day with Ostada Zohra, the warm-natured French schoolmistress. In addition to being an excellent and resourceful teacher always ready with answers, Fatiha often sees her comforting girls in the school hallways. Slight of build, funny, and strongly opposed to harsh discipline, Ostada Zohra is much liked by all the girls at school. She once asked Fatiha what she wanted to be in the future, and when Fatiha said, "a teacher," she screamed at her. "Never say that again! You must be more ambitious."

Since losing her mum, Fatiha has found solace in the company of Ostada Zohra, who has taken on a kind of surrogate mother role. Kind and affable, she is the only person in Fatiha's world who succeeds in wearing down her defensiveness. Spending time with her is one of the few things that bring her joy. The sight of Ostada Zohra's face, her smile, her voice - everything reminds Fatiha of her mother. One day, the French schoolmistress wore a blue crepe dress with red and yellow flowers, and Fatiha couldn't help but think it was her mother walking down the school corridor. For a brief moment, she allowed herself to imagine that her mother had come to visit her at school.

Fatiha sat alone on a bench made for two in the front row on the left side of the classroom—cited immediately after Ostada Zineb's desk. She had written her mother's name—Dawiya—all over the desk with a fountain pen, fitting the name alongside the numerous writings other students had scribbled on the same desk. A beam of sunlight streamed through one of the windows. Fatiha pulled out her Arabic notebook, which had a green marbleized cover with her name written in beautiful Arabic calligraphy. Despite the teacher's instructions, the notebook's pages were filled with pencil scrawls and no records of the lessons. Fatiha's eyes were so heavy that she struggled to keep them open, and she feigned interest by flipping through the pages, frowning.

Ostada Zineb takes off her kob. Every strand of her long, brown hair is pulled into a neat bun at the back of her head. Her glance sweeps through the room. She puts her purse on the desk piled high with students' exam copies. She bows her head, shuffles some papers, walks through the rows— taq, taq, taq—in her high heeled shoes, walks back to the front of the class, looks students up and down, opens a drawer in her desk, and again directs a searching look at students.

"Yesterday, I said you have to memorize Surat Al-Mulk. I will ask three or four students to recite it. Those who did not learn the assigned surat will be punished. There are no second chances."

Ostada Zineb's face was impassive as she spoke, and the students fidgeted in their seats. A girl at the back of the class tried to hide her face, but the teacher caught her movement out of the corner of her eye. The girl looked up with flushed cheeks, her eyes wide with fear. The teacher held her gaze.

Fatiha had not studied the Surat, and the thought of completing her homework was tedious. But she was not worried. After all, punishments were something that happened to other students, not her. She absentmindedly twisted a strand of her dark hair, watching as its wave unravelled. "Fatiha!" Ostada Zineb's voice loops across the room.

Fatiha feels a tautness in her stomach when she hears her name. The teacher's eyebrows raise towards her.

"Now. Stand up. Go to the board and recite Surat Al-Mulk." She says, her eyes sparkling, hostile.

Fatiha did not budge.

Ostada Zineb looks Fatiha in the eyes, and with a belligerent expression on her face, asks her to recite Surat Al-Mulk for the second time. Fatiha brushes off the hair lying on her face, then stands up, feeling the weight of everyone's eyes. She reluctantly leaves her desk and goes to the board with her heart pounding, the soft light through the windows casting shimmery radiance on her face.

Ostada Zineb's unwavering gaze made Fatiha feel even more self-conscious. A rush of thoughts overwhelmed her, and her throat constricted, making it difficult to speak. Finally, she managed to say in a quivering voice, "I didn't know we had to learn Surat Al-Mulk."

The teacher fixed Fatiha with her direct gaze. Her unblinking eyes wide and beautiful. The corners of her mouth twitching with a hint of a smile. "If you don't recite the Surat by heart, you'll have to wear ass ears," she says, her voice lilted with sarcasm.

The problem with Ostada Zineb was simple: Fatiha had disliked her ever since January when her mother died and her world fell apart. And Ostada Zineb disliked being disliked, especially by this intelligent and popular girl whom the other teachers seemed to favour. The ass ears were a deliberate attempt to humiliate Fatiha and break her spirit.

Fatiha heard a stifled chorus of giggles from the back of the room. She stole a quick glance over her shoulder and saw that all the girls were laughing, except for Amina Wahbi, who sat in the back row. Amina was the only girl in class who had tried to comfort Fatiha when her mother died, telling her, through her own tears, "You should not be sad. Your mother is in heaven. She is watching you from above." The words didn't bring much comfort, but they resonated deeply with her.

Ostada Zineb speaks again and Fatiha's heart begins to sink. "Ass ears! This is your punishment." With each repetition, the pitch of the teacher's voice climbs higher.

Tears pooled in Fatiha's grey-green eyes, and she felt a surge of shame. The thought of wearing the ass ears was an insult to her pride and dignity. She heard her own voice pleading with Ostada Zineb, "Please Ostada, find another way to punish me. Don't make me wear ass ears." But the words sounded distant and strange, as if they came from someone else.

Ostada Zineb almost felt a twinge of pity for Fatiha, but it quickly vanished. She walked over to her desk and rummaged through the drawers until she found the "ass ears," a homemade banner with the words "I am an ass" scrawled on brown paper. She held it up triumphantly, a cruel smirk on her face.

"Fatiha did not learn Surat Al-Mulk. She will wear ass ears and go in every classroom so as to give a good lesson to the other students." Ostada Zineb says without softening her tone.

The light seemed to glare mercilessly, and the silence was thick and heavy, like a physical weight pressing down on Fatiha. She became acutely aware of the silence, which seemed to hang oppressively in the air. Despite her sense of unreality, she maintained her composure, outwardly remaining polite and composed. But inside, she felt a storm of thoughts raging, thoughts of doing something outlandish like screaming or running up to and slapping the teacher. But she kept herself under control.

It is Fatiha against the teacher and she cannot have those ass ears around her head, for if she does, she will be known as the ass ears girl for the rest of her life. With the effort of one trying to walk through sludge in a dream, she tries to think of a way out of this problem.

Surat Al-Mulk. If she concentrates, maybe she can remember it. She has a remarkable memory. She prays for a miracle.

January 1st had been the only date that Fatiha had thought she would never forget. But now, she knew that today May 15th would join it, indelibly etched in her memory. Fatiha's bright, tired eyes danced around the classroom and she sees her classmates' faces, some scared, some blithe, some bored.

"Please Ostada, let me wear the ass ears in her place." Someone says in a shy but urgent voice.

A light seemed to flicker in Fatiha's eyes as she wondered if her prayer had been answered. She still resented God for taking her mother from her. But now, a girl whom she barely knew, Amina Wahbi, had offered to sacrifice herself for Fatiha's sake. Amina had a timid, candid face and big light-brown eyes. *Why is she constantly being kind to me?*

Ostada Zineb paces. She's rattled a little. At last she bursts out, "No, no, no! Fatiha did not do her homework. She is the one who must be punished." The pitch of her voice climbs higher with each new word.

Still, Amina stands up and looks at the teacher pleadingly. "Allah ykhlik Ostada," she says, choking back tears, her voice low and loaded with fright. She must have imagined Fatiha's feelings—the humiliation, the embarrassment. She must have realized how demoralizing; how outrageously idiotic this form of punishment is. And yet, here she is, willing to embrace it to save another girl who is not even her friend. Fatiha is deeply touched by this unsolicited kindness.

"No," Ostada Zineb affirms, her voice strong and insistent.

All hope is snuffed out in an instant. There are murmurs and some laughter, though they come to Fatiha in a muffled form.

Ostada Zineb was walking towards her, and Fatiha watched her warily, unsure what would happen next. Then, realization dawned on her, and dread began to rise up like a stone in her stomach. She was angry, afraid, and silent, her gaze fixed on the classroom door as if she was hoping for someone to come and rescue her.

A little voice in her head keeps urging her to run, but she knew that there was nowhere to go. She felt exhausted, but not too exhausted to fight. As Ostada Zineb tried to force the ass ears on her, Fatiha's heart pounded with fear and disgust. Then, without thinking, she whirled around and fled, her cheeks flushing red as she ran.

Ostada Zineb gaped in disbelief, then roared after her in anger and confusion. The class watched in shock as their teacher chased Fatiha around the room. Some students kept their eyes trained on the spectacle, while others looked away, too scared to look their teacher in the eye. Although they didn't like Ostada Zineb, they were too young and fearful to stand up to her.

Without a care for the consequences, Fatiha pushed past the desks and chairs, elbowing Khadija and squeezing past Milouda and Rabia. All the while, Ostada Zineb's face twisted in anger. Fatiha ran towards the door, desperate to escape the schoolmistress chasing her.

"You aren't coming anywhere near me," Fatiha blurts out, her voice quivering and pitched unnaturally high. The chase seems interminable. Fatiha feels as if she is caught in a terrible dream.

Aicha—a capricious girl with tumbling red hair and a freckled complexion—and Fatima—a fair-skinned girl with a skinny blond ponytail and an insipid smile—stand at the door of the classroom. Aicha and Fatima were Ostada Zineb's favourite students, but Fatiha disliked them both. In that moment, she felt an urge to grab Aicha's unruly hair and Fatima's silly ponytail and shake their heads as hard as she could. But the girls were staring at her as if she were a specimen under a microscope. Fatiha could hear their whispers and the things they were saying about her. They are waiting for her, ready to prevent her from getting out, as if she were a troublesome calf who has wandered away from the herd.

Fatiha looked them directly in the eyes, something she had never been able to do before. Despite her fear that they might grab her ankles, she forced herself to keep going, the sound of her own heartbeat filling her ears. She let out a bloodcurdling scream, her voice rising to match the sound of their jeers. Aicha and Fatima were wrestling with her on the ground, their hands and feet flying. Fatiha fought back with wild, animal energy, biting and hitting with a reckless abandon. All the while, she was aware of Ostada Zineb's watchful eyes from the back of the room. She pulled herself free from Aicha and Fatima and pushed past them, but Ostada Zineb continued to hurl insults and curses at her.

Fatiha turned the knob, pushed open the squeaky door, and ran out into the brightly-coloured corridor. The door banged against the shelf beneath the blackboard, stirring up a cloud of chalk dust. Fatiha ran at breakneck speed, her eyes blurry with tears and ink. She didn't think she would ever run so fast again

Fatiha ran across the corridors, her footsteps echoing as she descended the stairs to the school yard. She caught a glimpse of her mother's smiling face in the stairwell, and felt a sense of reassurance. She sped across the courtyard, her feet barely touching the ground as she raced away from the classroom and Ostada Zineb. It wasn't until she had gone a long way that she realized how far she had come.

"Ammi Hammad, open the door! Allah ykhlik, open the door. I want to go home." Fatiha cries, shaking from head to foot. She has no wish to speak, to express the bottled rage and pain she feels. She is pushed by one simple desire: to get away.

Ammi Hammad's face registered a mixture of emotions—surprise, concern, and maybe even a hint of anger. He unlocked the school gate without thinking and let her out. Fatiha crossed the street without looking left or right, vanishing into the maze of alleyways and markets that made up Hay Mohammadi. Within seconds, she was lost in the garden.

Fatiha was never caught by Ostada Zineb. Perhaps it was the adrenaline or her pride, or even a higher power, that protected her from the ultimate humiliation of wearing ass ears. But it was a narrow escape, and her pounding heart proved just how scared she had been. By the end of the morning, she was the most famous girl in Lala Lyacoute—the girl who refused to wear the ridiculous ass ears.

LOVE GROWS STRONGER IN DEATH

Going to Look for Adesua
MICHAEL CHIEDOZIEM CHUKWUDERA

I.

It was the first day of school in third term, primary four. After the assembly, my classmates and I marched into our class while the teachers headed for their own short meeting and prayers which they used to hold before they went to their classes to teach. We got into our class, and everybody looked new: all the boys had new hairstyles, the girls too. Some people who sewed new uniforms were showing themselves around class for everybody to see. But I was sad for nothing. I did not know how my body was doing because even as everybody was happy, talking about their holidays, I was quiet. Even when Obinna tried to hail me, I could not hail him back. I took the rag from Adaora, my seatmate after she had cleaned her seat to clean my own. There were only two of us in our row. Adesua, the girl who stayed in the middle, was not in school; she had told me last term that she will not come to our school again this term, but she changed her mind when I begged her. I had not seen her during the holidays because I travelled to Lagos to spend the holiday with my uncle and his family. I wondered if she had changed her mind. I decided that after school, I was going to go to their house to check if she had started another school. Her empty seat increased the space between me and my other seat mate, Adaora. And I did not want to talk with anybody, so I laid my head on the desk as my classmates kept discussing.

~

Soon, everybody became quiet as they heard the footsteps of teachers going to their various classrooms. The only noise that remained was the one being made by the birds which usually gather on top of the mango trees in the garden at the back of our class. Our teacher, Aunty Ese came in, and even the birds that were singing kept quiet. Osagie, our class prefect, hit the table five times, and we all stood up and greeted, "Good morning ma, we are happy to see you, may God bless you." Even though I joined in the greeting, I was not happy to see Aunty Ese.

~

She stood like a giant in front of our class with her black face and lips which are always painted red. The new weave-on which she fixed was the type that was like a cap and almost covers one eye. She used one of her hands to wave it from the front of her eye, she smiled and said, "How are you doing class?"

"We are fine, thank you, ma," we all responded.

"How are your parents?"

We answered that they were fine.

"I hope nobody lost any parents during the holidays?"

Everybody answered that they did not.

When it was time for her to ask us to sit down, Joy Obiegbunem raised her hands, "Aunty!"

And Aunty Ese's face changed, "Oh, my dear, but I passed your mother's shop today..."

"No," Joy said, "It is not my father or mother, it is Adesua."

Aunty Ese's eyes quickly came to our seat row and she saw that Adesua's seat was empty. "She is not in school today," Aunty Ese said, "What happened? I hope she is fine?"

"She is dead," Joy said and everybody shouted "Jesus!" I did not shout it with them. I did not believe it. I had already thought about Adesua that morning and told myself I was going to pass through their house today and ask her why she did not come to school. I watched Aunty Ese as she stood where she was, her shoulders raised up to show that she was surprised. Everybody in the class started talking about what Joy had said, it looked like some of our classmates had even heard it before, but I did not believe it. I was planning to go to her house after school to check if she had started another school.

"Joy, are you sure about what you are saying?" Aunty Ese said, when her mind came back.

"Yes," Joy said.

"Who told you?" Aunty Ese said.

"Her brother told me," Joy said, "the day that I went to their house to see her and ask her if she will still come to our school because she told us that her father said she will not come to our school again this term. When I went to their house and knocked on their door, her brother that used to come and carry her from school when we were in primary one came out. I told her that I wanted to see Adesua and he told me that she fell down the stairs when she was running...." And Joy stopped talking as if something entered her throat and she started crying more than she was crying before.

"Was that how she died?'

"Yes, they rushed her to the hospital and after some days, she died," Joy said.

By the time Joy finished telling us the story, some of my classmates' eyes were red and tears were rushing like water. But my eyes were not red because I did not even believe what they were saying. Even when Aunty Ese, our teacher who likes to flog people anyhow, walked slowly to her desk, sat down and bent her head on the desk and started crying, I did not cry because I did not believe. Was it not her that made Adesua tell her father that she would not come to our school again? Since we came into her class in primary three, we don't go for break; I was thinking about how we used to be inside the class and hear people in other classes playing drawing hearts on the floor to play suwe and others playing football during break time and she would say we should stay inside to read our books. She will only give us five minutes to go outside and buy food and if anybody stays past those five minutes, that person has entered trouble that day. Last term, Adesua came late after break time because the woman from whom she was buying snacks did not have change. That was the day Aunty Ese used vex to flog Adesua all over her body because she told her to bring her hands and Adesua was explaining. As she was swinging the slim cane all over Adesua's body and Adesua was dancing and crying, the cane landed on top of Adesua's eye and blood started coming out. All of us thought that Aunty Ese had blinded one of Adesua's eyes till we saw that it was on top of her eye brow that the blood was coming from. Was that not the day that Adesua told me that she will not come to our school this term? Even though Aunty Ese later apologised in front of the whole class, Adesua's mind was no longer in our school again. Aunty Ese loves flogging too much. What other teachers will warn their children to not do again, Aunty Ese will flog for. Even though she used to laugh with us sometimes and ask us about our parents and say she used to pray for us, she will still flog us for any small thing. When they promoted us to primary four, they promoted her with us because the children that are entering primary three went and started crying to their parents that the teacher in their new class is very wicked. So I said in my mind that this cry that Aunty Ese was crying today was not going to make me believe that Adesua is dead. After school, I knew I was going to go to Adesua's house to see her.

Soon, teachers from other classes started to come to our class. I did not know how, maybe somebody went to tell one of them, but it was as if the news was spreading outside our class, like fire on dry grass. Many of the teachers in our school started coming inside our class, even Mrs. Ehinomen, our headmistress. When they came, they saw our Aunty crying and many of my classmates too—so, they stood in front of our class looking at us and our teacher like people that were watching a sad film. It was as if they came to pour kerosene inside fire because as they stood there, the crying increased. Nobody was able to say anything but it was as if everything had been said. Some of the teachers that came to our class started crying with us. Uncle

Madu our housemaster, walked slowly to my row and sat on top of my desk. His head was just down as if he was thinking but he was not crying. My father always says that the worst a man can be is to be sad and a man does not cry. He would shout at me if I cried whenever my elder sister beats me and ask me to clean my eyes before he beats me more.

2.

Last term, a boy died in our school. They said he was crossing the wide main road at upper mission that leads to New Benin market and a tipper hit him. Everybody was sad, but our teachers did not gather in the boy's class even though some people who knew him cried too. But the boy was not popular in our school and when our teacher was told about the boy, she did not know who he was till our headmistress brought a picture from our last graduation ceremony which had the boy in it.

~

Adesua's case was different because she was the fastest runner in our school's inter-house sport last term. She was in my house, yellow house, and Uncle Madu was our housemaster. During practice, he tested all of us in different sports, and put us in the ones he saw we knew how to do. That was when he chose Adesua as one of the people who will represent our house in running and gymnastics. He used to say she had the body of an Olympian because she ran so fast and twisted her body into different shapes as if it was easy. She would bend her body backwards and use her hand to hold her self in place as soon as her head is about to touch the ground, then she would move her hands to touch her legs and her shape would be like a tyre. Sometimes, she would almost roll. She used to spread her legs, straight, one backwards, the other forward, the way they do on TV. Sometimes, almost everybody gathered to watch her as she did those things. Then on our inter house sports day, she came first in the 100-metres and 200-metres race, and also the high jump even beating some people in primary five. From that day, everybody in our school came to know that there was a girl called Adesua.

3.

It's already past One O'clock in the afternoon and they have just rang the closing bell. It was not a sweet day in school at all. Our class was too quiet. Our teacher was teaching us with a heavy voice. If you heard her, you would know that she had truly cried and it made me know she was not forming that cry in the morning. It was a real cry. The news had touched everybody because they all love Adesua. Even me that did not believe the news, I was not able to talk. By eleven O'clock, the break bell had rang and for the first time in as long as we could remember, our teacher asked all of us to go for break. Everybody was surprised. That was the only time when there was a noise in class today, as everybody rushed out of the class, most of my classmates were happy as if they had forgotten the news in the morning. But after we returned from break and saw that Aunty Ese's eyes were red, the sadness came back again, but still, I did not believe that Adesua was dead.

Now, I am walking home along with some of my school people. After we pass the gate, we divide into two. Some people go to their houses through the road on the right and some others go through the road on the left. Adesua used to go with us to the road on the left. Her street is two streets before my own. Sometimes, I can pass through her street and come out in another street that leads to my own street. But that road is farther than the direct road. But I will take the farther road because I am going to see Adesua in her house. When I see her, tomorrow I will go to school and announce to everybody that she is alive.

Just before we got to Ajayi street where Adesua's father's house is, we see many people gathered; they are looking at a big dead snake which a man is holding up on a stick. Some of my schoolmates stop to watch but I will not stop. I am going to see Adesua, so I can beg her to come back to our school, and tell her how everybody thinks she has died and how Aunty Ese has been crying for her. I wonder how she would feel about this. She would probably be surprised and feel sorry for Aunty Adesua. She is like that, she has a mind of pity.

The staircase is dark as I get there. I have not climbed it before but from downstairs I have seen Adesua standing upstairs many times and I know which of the flats she lives in. I have already used my eyes to calculate which step I will climb and which door I will knock. The stairs are cool but it is dark because there is no window and you have to pass through a dark passage to get to it. The only place where light is coming from is the top wall where some holes are designed. Some like circles, some triangles, some stars. It is as if different suns are shining through each one of them as I look up. I am also seeing dust dancing through the lines of sunlight as I climb the stairs.

I knock on the door, the first time and nobody answers. I knock again and I hear her brother's voice ask from inside, "Who be dat?!" and I answer, "Na me!" He asks again, "Who you be?" and I say, "Adesua classmate." Everywhere is now quiet in the staircase. Maybe the boy is not going to open the door for me. I want to go downstairs, but another mind is telling me to knock again, another is telling me to wait. As my different minds are busy telling me different things, I hear somebody coming to the door and then, the person opens the door and it is Adesua's brother. It is as if the resemblance between him and Adesua has increased. His lips and nose are red and long like her own and even his eyes are shining as he is looking at me.

"Good afternoon." I say.

"Good afternoon," he says.

I don't know how to say what I want to say.

"You come see us?" He says.

"Yes," I say, thinking of how to ask him if it is true that Adesua has died.

"Oya nah, come inside," he says shifting for me to enter.

As I enter the house, the first thing I see on the balcony is Adesua's picture on a small table rounded with flowers. From nowhere, I gather my mind and I turn to Adesua's brother and ask him, "So na true say Adesua done die?"

4.

My legs are heavy as I reach our home. It was as if I would not reach at all when I was coming. As I pass through the passage, I can hear my father practising Osita Osadebe's *Makojo, anyi ga-ebi oo* with his piano inside his room. But I go through the passage into my room. With force, I kick out my shoes from my legs and one of the legs flew towards the window, the other towards my father's bookshelf which he kept in our room. And I fall on top of my bed and started crying all the cry that I did not cry in school because I did not believe that Adesua had died. I wish I could still continue not believing it but her brother couldn't have lied to me. All these things are going up and down in my mind as I am crying. I look up and I see my father standing next to my bed and I try to control the cry but I cannot. I am crying and having hiccups. I know my father hates to see me cry; I know he will rather beat me than console me because for him, a man cannot cry, only women. So I try more to control the crying when I see him. But the more I try to control the cry, the more it comes out. When my father sees that it is not an ordinary cry, he asks me what happened and I tell him while I am still crying that my friend who is my classmate in school died when I travelled to Lagos for holidays, and I continue crying.

For the first time in my life, my father is not telling me to not cry, as a man, but he comes to sit next to me and hugs me. I feel as if they poured cold water on my body even though my father's body was warm. The surprise made me cry more.

"It's okay, it's okay my son," he says.

I try again to control my crying but I can not control it and so I keep crying in my father's arms. If Adesua could die like this, I know now for the first time in my life that anybody can also die without expecting it.

LOVE GROWS STRONGER IN DEATH

Aubade in Sagamu 🅔

ENIT'AYANFE AYOSOJUMI AKINSANYA

It pounded like hell in Sagamu on the same day two bombs exploded near a crowded vegetable market far away in Maiduguri. It was like the sky was a strangely bloated belly and someone had sliced it open with a dagger. The roads became riverbeds and houses shrank in size as sky met earth. The roaring in the gutters and on the roofs deafened people, and intermittent growls shook the buildings. Above these noises, Ini heard a fresh salvo of fists on his bedroom door, so loud that he was forced to finally open it.

His mother stood there glaring at him. "You locked yourself in there since yesterday evening!" She waved a metal spoon dripping with sauce. "Nobody could make you talk or come out of there. Maybe now that your friend is here, you will talk."

"Thank you, mummy," the last voice Ini wanted to hear said, and its owner stepped out of the shadowed hallway to walk into the room.

"*Káàbọ̀ jàre,* my son," the woman said. "Ask him why he turned himself into a prisoner since he returned from the hostel. Ask him why he has been crying."

"I will, mummy."

She ran a withering gaze over Ini, turned and disappeared back into the kitchen. Ini closed and bolted the door.

His friend, Yanju, had perched himself on the bed, back against the wall. Ini sat next to him and trussed a pillow between his own legs.

"They said nobody died," he said.

"That's what I heard too," Yanju replied. "My mum forced all of us to watch the news."

Ini swung him a glance. "She did? Then it must really be serious."

"It is."

The louvres rattled beside them, under the strong sheets outside. Ini reached up to pull the curtains closed. The penumbra settled over them like a dark blue blanket.

"Are you okay, Ini?"

Ini chewed on his lower lip. "I heard my dad fuming at the screen before NEPA took the light. I think he didn't consider Jonathan's state of emergency approach strong enough to protect Nigerians. He kept yelling, 'Only the northern regions? What about the east? What about the southwest? What about us?'"

"I think the attacks are focused on the northern regions, Ini. At least for now."

"True." Ini pressed his hands to his face. "Do you know they killed a girl in Jigawa with a stray bullet? I'm sure she didn't even know those that were shooting at each other or why."

Yanju shook his head. "She was a little girl. She couldn't have understood."

Ini started drumming on the pillow. "Then my dad's fears are right. Who's to even say it won't spread down to other regions? Their name means 'Western education is forbidden', doesn't it? There are people going to formal schools in other parts of the country. I just finished from one."

His hands started to shake. Yanju seized them.

"What's going on, Inioluwa? Do I really have to ask one more time?"

Ini wrenched his hands free. "Leave me alone!"

Yanju recoiled.

Ini resumed his drumming and snarled. "Why did you come here?"

"Inioluwa, we've finished our SSCE exams. We have all returned home from our schools. It's normal for me to want to see you after so long."

"So you entered the rain?"

"Temitope drove me here. Besides, it was only drizzling when we set out."

Ini fell silent. Then he started laughing, shoulder-jerking cackles that made the pillow on his thighs bounce.

"You didn't take weed in your hostel, did you?" Yanju asked, a joshing lilt in his voice.

Ini tried to find his friend's eyes in the dark. "If I told you I did not, would you believe me?"

Yanju nodded. "I would, Inioluwa. I would."

"I did not," Ini said, then started to cry. "I—I tried it again today, Yanju. I tried it again today."

Yanju rested his occiput against the wall and cupped his eyes in the hollows of his fists. "What did you use this time?"

Ini blabbered something.

"Well, speak up!" Yanju yelled.

"I didn't use any sharp objects!" Ini yelled back.

"Of course!" Yanju threw up his hands. The storm outside may have muffled their voices but the dimness enclosing them in the room amplified their anguish. "Your wrists are tired from all the cutting, and I'm also tired of supporting the stories you tell about 'school accidents' each time your parents worry over the scars when you come home for the holidays. I can't join you to lie to them anymore!"

Ini's voice had shrunken. "At least now, there are no more holidays. I've written my final exams."

"Isn't it a miracle that you stayed alive that long!" Yanju's voice was still strong.

Ini pressed his hand over Yanju's mouth. "Lower your voice, Yanju, my dad is napping in the next room and my mum might be in the sitting room now. Or worse, her ears pressed to this door listening!"

Yanju shoved Ini's hand off but tamped down. "What on earth did you use this time?"

Ini hung his head. "I stashed a bottle of Omo detergent solution under my bed before I opened the door. I was just about to drink it when Mummy pounded on the door."

Yanju's face was half-illuminated by the dim light through the window crack, revealing a smile that seemed both genuine and mysterious.

"This is about Maleek."

"No! Not just him. Everything, Yanju. Everything. I need to end it all. My journey with Maleek only proved that I will never be happy being like this, because no one will love me like this."

"So you locked yourself indoors for nearly a day to come round to poisoning yourself because a guy you crushed on in school left you for a girl."

"It was not a *crush*, oga." Ini's voice had sharpened again. "Don't make this sound so trivial. Maleek was everything. Everything. I once believed he felt that way about me, too. I thought he was just scared of people catching us in the hostel. But now, I know he finds me disgusting."

"And thus, the end of your life began," Yanju said.

"Don't use your poetic lines on me, oga. Besides, what's with the smirk? You really think I wouldn't have gone through with it, don't you?"

"Oh, no. I totally believe you would have. It's becoming a familiar sight. You remember, right?"

Ini buried his face in the pillow, trying to hide from the memory unfurling in his head. In his early childhood, during Christmas, on the night he and Femi, Yanju's brother, play-wrestled at Yanju's place, Ini had grown hard in his boxers and Femi had untangled himself from him with a heavy, quizzical stare. Ini had run home, through the dusty coldness and screaming children and whistling firecrackers, and cried for a full week afterwards. Then, as the days and the fire in his loins grew, he started slashing his wrists with blades. He hid it well from everybody, but not from Yanju, who always seemed to see right through him. Ini cut himself more often after he fell for Maleek, often enough for his parents to finally notice, and that was when the lies started. Yanju became an unwilling accomplice, forced to choose between his loyalty to Ini and his obligation to Ini's parents.

Yanju shook his head now. "What just amuses me about it all is why you are certain Omo detergent solution will be the one to finally do the job."

Ini raised his head and looked away. "I Googled it on the internet with my new phone."

Yanju nodded. "Excellent. This mobile phone thing that Obasanjo introduced will one day be the end of us all."

"Stop sounding like a conspiracist, oga. I could have also used Daddy's desktop computer."

"But you wouldn't, since you are an *olódo*. Too dense to know how to wipe out your search history. Is that not why you dare not browse those porn sites with his computer?"

Ini hurled the pillow at him. "*Orì ẹ ò pé!*" He was cackling, new tears joining the dried lines on his cheeks. He rained blows on Yanju, who ducked and laughed along.

"Imagine him coming home from work one evening and deciding to use his computer, and he's seeing 'White Twink barebacked by a Black Hung

Janitor' across the screen." Yanju was holding the pillow as a shield from Ini's fists.

Ini stopped punching and doubled over. "Stop, you mad child!"

"With graphic images to suffice!" Yanju said.

"I would be so sunk!" Ini threw his head back to guffaw.

"Exactly." Yanju was crying, too. He coughed. "And everyone would know about you, and then you would be in real trouble and finally have a good reason to kill yourself." He paused. "Not this one, you fool. Not because your first love left you on the brink of passing out of school. What if he's not even gay after all? Inioluwa, you were the star student in your school; you are smarter than all of this."

"I know."

"Should we tell Mummy and Daddy what happened?"

Ini went stiff. "I would rather die than tell them I'm gay."

The noises outside had diminished. Yanju scrambled to his knees by the window and parted the curtains. He pressed his nose to the louvres and peered through. "I think the rain stopped."

"Is it because I'm fat?" Ini called from behind him.

"What?" Yanju crawled back to his side.

"The girl Maleek left me for is slim."

"You idiot. Come here." Yanju pulled him into a side embrace. "We talked about this. It's not the size of your body; it's the size of their brain."

"Easy for you to say something so corny," Ini snapped. "You are slender and handsome. You are dating a doctor, and he treats you like a glass cup. Nobody even looks at me unless they want to laugh at my rolling body."

His arm still around Ini, Yanju scrunched up his nose and sniffed the air. "What's that? What's smelling here? Oh, it's just jealousy."

Ini resumed thumping him, and they both shrieked into the rain-washed afternoon.

~

Yanju stayed till nightfall. He joined the family at the table for a supper of pounded yam and egusi soup with chunks of fried beef. The petrichor wafting in through the lifted louvres and window net was so strong in his nose that he wanted to suck his fingers dry of the palm oil, go out and dig out clumps of rain-soggy earth to eat instead. Power was still out; the power company would need at least five more days for the wires to dry up first. That was their story. A rechargaeble radio lamp hung from the wall, near the photos, and cast its white beam over the room.

"I just hope all these policies this man is blindly introducing because of these terrorism attacks will not come around to bite us in the ass someday," Ini's father was saying.

"They won't, sir. President Jonathan is humane and wise," Yanju responded. In other homes, it would have been considered rude—to talk after an adult had spoken. But here, Yanju was at home. He was more than a child. He was their son's guide, the only one who could ever get Ini to be cheerful, who could ever shorten Ini's silences.

"I think the flowing dirt water out there has ebbed," Ini said, glancing through the glass doors. Lightning flashed and showed the earth and the swaying trees.

"It's getting late, my dear Yanju," Ini's mother said. "Or are you passing the night here?"

Yanju shifted in his chair. "Actually, ma, there is a vigil at my church, and I don't know if Inioluwa can come with me." He glanced at Ini who looked away.

"Why not," the father said, licking his fingers and pulling up his sleeves with his free hand. "What's he doing at home except crying?"

"Daddy," Ini subtly objected.

"Did I lie? Eh? Crying waa-waa as if he's the first to finish from secondary school."

The mother laughed. "*Ẹ má jẹ n só'ta, Bàbá Ini,*" she said. She faced Yanju. "He will go with you o. If not for the fact that we don't have our vigils on Tuesdays, he would be in church right now. I am tired of his crying. I know you told us he was crying because he's missing his schoolmates already. But I feel there is more. And maybe he can talk to Jesus if he can't talk to us."

Yanju smiled into his soup.

~

After his father dropped them at the junction of the church around 8 that night and drove away into the wet night, Inioluwa wondered if an imaginary friend would truly listen as his mother had said, when even those who were not nebulous figments of imagination did not seem to be listening. And he knew Yanju was lying about the vigil service. An improper fraction of relief and curiosity filled him when Yanju hailed an okada, reeled out the destination address, and asked him to climb on. Speechless, Ini clambered onto the pillion. Yanju climbed after him, his lean muscles digging into Ini's supple flesh, and they sped away.

The bike man stopped in front of a gated compound along Ayepe, on the outskirts of town, and tilted forward for them to climb down. Crickets filled the damp black air with their chirpings. They contested with the rumble of the power generator coming from inside the compound. The bike man left his headlamp on to doublecheck as Yanju paid him, and Ini glimpsed a pink and cream bungalow in the half-lit compound.

"Where is this place?" He gasped. "Don't tell me..."

Yanju nodded. "Yes, Temitope's house. The state university hospital gave him these quarters. Exquisite, isn't it?"

"Your mouth like exquisite."

They laughed as the bike man vroomed away.

~

Temitope welcomed them with a smile and the aroma of jollof rice drifting out of his kitchen. His TV was on, displaying a loud Chinese movie. Ini sat on the sofa closest to the electronic shelf and tried to concentrate on the flashing swords and billowing dresses on the screen while Temitope and Yanju fondled and kissed on the settee across the room.

"The rice is burning o," he finally said when he heard the zzzz of a zipper flying open. The room echoed with laughter. They ate the jollof rice with fried fish and glasses of Coke. Yanju fell asleep on the carpeted floor. Soon, Temitope got up and asked Ini to follow him into his bedroom.

"For what?" The words were out of Ini's mouth before he realized he had whispered them.

"I just want to show you something for Yanju," Temitope whispered back. "I don't want him to know about it."

He took Ini by the hand and led him in. There was no light in the bedroom and, at first, Ini wanted to run back. But Temitope calmed him down. He grabbed something from the top of what looked like a round plastic table propped against a wardrobe. Ini waited for Temitope to hit him with the object in his hand, like villains did in movies, but when Temitope opened it, it was a laptop. The activation theme hummed through the room.

"What—what's that?"

In the bluish-white screen light, Temitope looked amused. "A laptop."

"Of course, I know what it is. I'm just—I…"

"Why don't you sit on the bed?" Temitope said. He pushed Ini gently until he landed on the downy mattress.

Ini felt his back grazing the bed, Temitope climbing him, prying his thighs apart with his knees. Falling on him. Ini froze. Temitope was tucking his hand into Ini's trousers, pulling them down, hitching up Ini's legs and pinning him down with his own swollen nakedness. And even though Temitope's lips had claimed his own, Ini still asked, in a small voice, "Is what you want to show me still on the laptop?"

"Shh." Temitope leaned up and placed a finger across Ini's lips. The laptop lay forgotten on the table. "Is it painful? Should I go slowly?"

But Ini didn't want him to go in, in any manner. With each movement Temitope made, Ini felt as if a razor was poking into him, shredding his insides, drawing blood. His body was a dry log. His scream was a buried ghost in his mouth. Warm tears tickled the sides of his eyes.

"Do you feel like going to the toilet?" Temitope suddenly asked.

Ini did. His insides churned. This pain had never happened before. But he would rather die. Die under this man, die in his bed.

He shook his head, clenched his lips, closed his eyes and dug his fingers into the mattress as Temitope's panting got faster.

~

At first, when Yanju woke up, everywhere was too dark for him to rally his senses immediately. The ceiling fan was still whirling, but the television had been switched off. Then his nose warmed to the smell of the house. He groped for the bulb switch but couldn't find it. Groggy, traipsing, but instinctive, he made his way towards Temitope's bedroom.

And then he saw them.

He saw them through the doorless frame. He made no sound. He walked back to the sitting room and lay on the settee, his eyes squeezed shut, that they might think he was still asleep.

~

Weeks crept past. Yanju did not visit. He did not come online on 2go. Ini's heart glided up into his mouth. Did Yanju know? Did Temitope tell him? The days of silence from Yanju were too loud, and they weighed on Ini's shoulders. Something had to give.

He appeared at Yanju's house one afternoon and found him running towards the kitchen. He followed him and watched as Yanju stirred beans in a pot on fire.

"Old man, what were you doing?"

"I was writing a poem." Yanju replied. He stretched out the stained, yellow, plastic ladle towards Ini.

Ini touched it and licked his finger. "A little more pepper."

Yanju grabbed the jar of ground pepper.

"Let me see," Ini said.

"No one is allowed to see my poems," Yanju said. "And since when have you been interested in my writing?" He laughed.

Ini shook his head and leaned against the slightly sooty wall. "I will never be able to understand writers. Why you feel the need to write."

He saw a shadow play across Yanju's face.

"Even we writers don't understand ourselves," Yanju said, gazing through the window.

"Is it true that you people must never date or marry each other?"

"Yes, it's true."

"Oh dear."

Yanju covered the pot with a clatter. "I thanked God every day that Temitope is not a writer."

The air darkened. A radio somewhere out on the street crackled out: "…in the hope that some Nigerians survived the inopportune Dana air crash…"

Yanju's eyebrows tautened. "'Inopportune'. What sort of pretentious word is that?"

Ini sat on the edge of the low table, over which old newspapers had been wrapped. "So, what is Temitope?"

"He's a chub chaser."

"What's he doing with you then? You're slim."

" *Was* doing with me. I don't know." Yanju shrugged. "Love, I guess. He couldn't help himself apparently."

Ini nodded. It was time. "My mother asked me if we were fighting."

"What did you tell her?"

Ini shrugged. "I told her we got caught up in the pressure of waiting for our WASSCE results."

Yanju burst into laughter. "I don't accept that she swallowed that."

The silence thickened.

"I let him enter me," Ini said. "That night. I could have shouted and woken you up. But I remained silent. I did a stupid thing, a terrible thing, and I am very sorry."

Yanju shifted a knife across the table. "I know."

"You know?"

"Yes."

Ini sprang up. "So, you were just waiting around for me to mention it before you tell me? What kind of friend are you?"

Yanju's eyes widened. "What? Are you serious right now? What kind of friend are *you*?" He stopped, as if that was not what he had wanted to say.

Ini spread out his hands. "Well, forgive me. I was caught up in the middle of a situation I didn't understand and still don't understand!"

"You slept with him!"

"He raped me!"

Yanju fidgeted with the pot handles. Ini walked to his side.

"Can't you see? He forced me. I didn't even enjoy it. I bled for days."

Yanju turned. "I can't face you right now. Please leave."

Ini folded. It took all of his strength to walk out without another word.

~

Resentment yawned between them, but there was enough in the country to occupy their minds. January of 2013 was a stretch of mixed surprises. The Nigeria Army killed thirteen terrorists in a showdown, and, in reprisal, Boko Haram raided a police station in Song, laying lives to waste.

Ini's father hurried into the house on one of those days that NEPA left power on. "You people don't watch the news in this house," he railed. "All the time, films, films."

"The films are more believable than the news," Ini's mother retorted.

His father grabbed the remote and clicked away. NTA came on, news montage flickering across the screen. The president had just announced an end to the fuel subsidy scheme and members of the Nigeria Labour Congress had taken to the streets with placards and tree branches.

"See? See what I was telling you about this man? Like there was not enough heat in the country already. How does he expect these labourers to afford fuel for their work now? Will their cars and engines drink water? Will this not affect everybody?"

Ini browsed for more news online. Boko Haram were wiping out civilians in Damboa, Borno, the state Maleek lived in with his family. Ini's heart jumped. Visions invaded his nights, of Maleek lying in a stream of blood, his head apart from his body. And on some of those nights, Ini woke up screaming and sweating.

~

Another January came along, but the New Year news pleased Nigerians this time. President Goodluck Jonathan passed a law against homosexual unions in the country. Anyone caught clamouring for such a matrimony would face long years in prison. But the citizens, unsatisfied, formed their own judiciary and executive boards. Women caught with other women in bed across all regions of the country were dragged out and burnt on the street while everyone threw curses and more petrol at the shrieking, blackening bodies. The same thing went for men found in such positions. It was as if the announcement of the law unleashed everybody's malice towards homosexuals. It was this news that finally bridged the distance between Ini and Yanju. Ini found himself running to Yanju's house. He found him home alone.

"I'm so glad you are not dating Temitope anymore," he said, bending over to catch his breath. "Imagine what they would have done to you if they found out."

Yanju gave a smile so sad. "At least, since the terrorist attacks and blow-ups did not unite us as a country, this hatred will. We just have to be more careful, that's all."

There was light. A scrawny boy was yelling on the TV screen, "Did they caught me? Did they caught me?" He was one of the boys raided and arrested at a hotel in Lagos by the Nigerian police, "for engaging in homosexual practices."

"Catch him doing what?" Ini asked. "And what kind of English is that?"

Yanju laughed.

Back home, Ini's father ranted. "Wait, did the insurgents not just declare an official war against the government and the Christians? Is this irrelevant law the next thing? What is this man doing? What is the nation's priority? Have they found the kidnapped schoolgirls?"

"He is doing the right thing, Bàbá Inioluwa," his mother said. "Those sodomists are just as evil as the killers out there. Imagine that one of them manages to get to our son." She shuddered. "Leave the man alone. Did he not grant amnesty to the Niger Delta militants to join the fight against the insurgents? Leave the man alone, he's not a fool."

Ini's world started to break.

~

Yanju gained admission into University of Ibadan. Ini also gained admission into Obafemi Awolowo University in Ile-Ife. The university towns were not far from each other, but their friendship was already stilted and neither visited the other. Ini started replying Yanju's messages late, if he replied at all. He tried to stay off boys, but his heart was always faster than his brain. He joined a Christian Fellowship, where he and a host of soul winners routinely went from hostel door to hostel door and out into the street to hand out salvation fliers to people walking past. During his holidays in Sagamu, he avoided Yanju's house and was often out attending spiritual retreats. He wanted a fresh start with people untainted by the flashbacks of his darkest secrets.

~

Yanju finally took the hint and stopped reaching out. His life took on a spur. He met Nwanna on Facebook. Nwanna was a third-year English Education student at Nsukka. He had 'Catholic Religious' on his bio. He had "Professional Artist" there too, but his news feed was crammed with posts shared from political profiles and sites with sanctimonious diatribes against atheists and human rights' activists. There were also a few one-liners about how the anger of God against the homosexuals of Sodom was justifiable. When Yanju asked him what type of artist he was, Nwanna logged out of Messenger for days. Then he came back and asked to meet Yanju.

They met at a restaurant in Ibadan, soft jazz in the background, huge glass panes shielding them and their scrupulous chat as they ate and drank.

"I can't believe you actually travelled down to Ibadan," Yanju said, forking fried rice into his mouth.

Nwanna had only a bottle of Sprite before him, which he sipped through a straw. He leaned across the table; his extra-long eyelashes fluttered as he smiled behind his glasses. "Nobody knows me here."

It was the first thing he said when Yanju took him to his apartment at Agbowo. *Nobody knows me here.* It was as if the sentence gave Nwanna grace, some legitimacy, because as Yanju grabbed his buttocks and felt their bouncy softness, he quickly stripped Yanju of his clothes and pushed him onto the bed. He undressed himself too, down to his underpants, until the only thing Yanju could see of Nwanna was the long swell of his penis. Nwanna climbed him, his hand on Yanju's hip, and slowly guided Yanju into himself. Yanju gasped, feeling himself tucked deeply into Nwanna. He threw his head back against the pillow and shut his eyes. He tried not to think of Sagamu. He tried not to think of Ini. He grasped Nwanna's waist, felt its suppleness, the practised fluidity with which it moved, and knew— just knew—that Nwanna might publicly condemn homosexuals, but he had gay sex often.

The moans rose. Yanju was lifting his hip underneath Nwanna's relentless wet warm squelching hole, slamming himself into its passionate pucker to match the rocking, currents of pleasure zapping through his groin and nipples, when a girl suddenly screamed from behind the window. "Homo! Homo! *Chi m o*! Come and see them!"

In a flash, and just as Yanju was cumming, Nwanna sprang up and yanked the horrified Yanju up to his feet. Yanju hunched over. Semen splattered onto the floor.

"Quick, get into that!" Nwanna, his eyes glittering, was pointing to the five-foot wardrobe by the bed.

"No one was supposed to be in the compound!" Yanju whispered fiercely. "It's the holidays and I locked the gates!"

"Holy Mother of God!" Nwanna hissed back. "Get in there!"

People were banging on the door, baying, asking to see the offenders of the law. Yanju scooted into the four-feet wardrobe, naked as he had been on the day of his birth. The odour of plywood stuffed his nostrils, and Nwanna twisted the lock after him, twice.

He heard Nwanna pull on his clothes, belt clasp clinking, and open the door. He heard his neighbours storm in. A dude in Agric department who woke everyone up with his Arabic chants every morning asked Nwanna where Yanju was. In the growing heat of the wardrobe, Yanju heard Nwanna say that Yanju was his friend who had handed his keys over to him before he travelled home so he, Nwanna, could bring girls there to fuck. They asked him to show them this particular girl. They said if he was unable to produce the girl he had been naked with, they were going to parade him around town, with whips lashing at his body and stones pelting him from the hands of everyone in Agbowo. That was when Yanju heard the insane scuffle, then a crash, then somebody shrieking, "Don't let him get away! Chase him! Catch him!" Then—

Silence.

Utter silence.

Soon, the air in Yanju's wardrobe thinned out. He started beating against the door, no longer afraid that they would hear and see him. He beat and beat against the door. But no one heard. No one came to let him out. All of them had gone after Nwanna, bent on Nwanna's blood. It happened fast. He began to scream. He began to yell and convulse. To sputter like a flame about to disappear. His fists grazed the wardrobe door limply. He called out weakly, "Nwanna, I can't breathe. Nwanna, please." Until his blows and efforts completely failed, completely slowed down.

Finally, against the wood, he went still. Never to wake again.

~

Ini was in class when the call came in. But he didn't pick it. When the lecturer walked out, his phone rang out again. He answered it.

It was Yanju's mother.

"They found your friend in his wardrobe," she said. "Naked. Completely naked. He was suffocated to death." She sounded like she was commenting on the weather.

"Ma? I didn't hear you, ma."

The woman went on, her voice unbroken, unrising. "They had to break the door down. They found my boy naked. Cold. Nobody took him to the hospital. They were afraid to touch him, but they called us. When we got there, we couldn't touch our son either. It didn't seem like it was the moral thing to do, to touch him."

"Yanju was naked?"

The call jammed. Ini took a bike to his hall, took a cold bath, and went for his evening choir rehearsals. He paid attention to his score sheets more than ever and, for the first time, raised his voice to an impeccable tenor pitch, drawing stares and thumbs-up from people. He nodded at them, grateful that they were present at this particular time. He filled his mind with the song. He was determined not to think of anything else, not to give room for the impossible in his mind.

~

They carried Yanju's body home to Sagamu and kept it in the mortuary. Before Ini's father parked his car in front of Yanju's parents' house, Ini imagined that they had brought the wrong body home, and that someday he and Yanju would laugh at the silliness, the mistake of it all. He stepped out with his parents and walked into the house, waiting to see Yanju inside so that the nightmare could fade. His mother went straight to Yanju's mother and held her close, rocking her gently like one would a baby, both women sobbing. Ini looked away. He saw one of Yanju's aunts spreadeagled on the floor, holding Yanju's photo frame to her breasts and ululating. Her wrapper had rolled up and Ini could see her tights, nude in tone, so that they blended with the colour of her thighs. He wished the woman would shut the hell up. Did she not know it was not true, that Yanju was not dead? That Yanju could not be dead? Death happened to people you didn't know. Like people up in the north. Not to people with whom you grew up. Not to people who wrote the first pages of your heart with you. Not to people who chose you over the love of their life.

"But what happened?" Ini heard his father asking Yanju's father. "Who did the neighbours say locked him in there? Why?"

Ini squirmed. When hatred and violence rocked the country, it was usually because of terrorists, was supposed to be because of terrorists, not because of normal people. Who put Yanju in a closet and killed him?

"Inioluwa." It was Yanju's mother, rising, gathering her wrapper around her broad waist. "Come with me."

She took him to Yanju's room, hoisted down a huge box from a shelf nailed to the wall, and placed it in front of Ini. It was full of Yanju's poetry books. "We are going to burn everything else," she said. She patted his shoulders, turned, and gently closed the door behind her.

The first thing Ini saw when he opened the first book in the pile was a square piece of paper Sellotaped to the inner flap.

Lately, I have begun to have some confusing feelings about us. I was not even sure who I was mad at that night. But now I am sure. It was me. I have always loved you. I just didn't realise early enough that it was you my heart beat for. And seeing you pine like that over Maleek, and then watching you and Temitope that night all broke something in me—and woke me up. Since primary 4, it's been us together, looking out for each other, in one bond. It's always been you and me, Ini.

The bells started to peal in Ini's head then. He flipped the page and another paragraph stared back at him.

This is my note to you, Inioluwa.

I have always been afraid of your reaction. I'm a coward, yes. But I have a feeling that you use anger as a mask. I could tell you, and then you would never speak to me again. You would remember that night, that incident, how I turned away even after I saw him on you, and you would hate me afresh. That was why I kept away from you, not because I was mad at you, but because I didn't want to give you a new chance to be mad at me.

Writing from the dead. It left Ini on the edge of the bed, pillars crashing inside him. A ferocious hunger seized him. He read sixteen poems before he got to the one that stayed with him. It was titled "Aubade in Sagamu".

> *Silence is the tape with which I measure the guilt that squeezes out half my story and impregnates the night*
>
> *Light will be the morning,*
>
> *but birds building boundaries*
>
> *like nests of shyness will sing with sealed beaks*
>
> *I never needed words to understand you*
>
> *but when there are no more words to me from you, let this dawn sing, sing me a last farewell home*
>
> *Home, home to you*
>
> *to this place, where our story began—may it never end*

The lettering on the paper melted. He saw the wet splotches landing on the paper before he tasted the salt of his tears. He stuck the open book to his chest and let his eyes stream.

Ini, this shouldn't interrupt your life.

"My life is changed forever, Yanju," Ini said into the empty room, as if someone were listening. "I cannot come back from this."

Assure me you'll be okay. That you don't need me. For once in your life.

"I cannot. I cannot form the words. They have ruined us. *I* have ruined us."

I love you, you idiot child.

"Nine years, Yanju. Nine years and you didn't for once say this to me. You are the idiot."

He sprawled across Yanju's bed, the page of the poem still pressed to his heart, buried his nose in Yanju's pillow. And wailed.

~

"You won't come?" his mother asked the following week, her face ashen and sceptical. She went on strapping on her sandal. She was giving him a chance to say he was cracking a stupid joke.

"I won't," he said.

She paused. "What?"

"I don't want to see Yanju's body wrapped in sheets and lowered into a grave. What made that body Yanju is gone, and it is now in my heart."

His father sighed. "Inioluwa, it's hard, I know. But I think you have to pay him your last respects. He is your friend." He rubbed his eyes. "Was."

"I don't need to attend a funeral before I can pay him my last respects, Daddy. We still talk."

His parents swapped nervous glances. He picked another of Yanju's manuscripts and opened to a fresh poem. His sudden interest in the written word was both frightening and exhilarating. What kind of adults went to such a funeral anyway? It was going to be a quiet, private affair, with only friends, classmates, and cousins in attendance. The parents were not going to be there, because it was taboo in Sagamu for parents to attend their children's burial. Why were his own father and mother going then? Had Yanju not been like a child to them?

He knew what to do to honour him. He had to learn how to grieve him on his own. Words were swirling now in his belly, fast, a terrible terrifying force.

"Mummy, Daddy, I have something to tell you."

They waited, a scoffing gleam in their eyes, as though they wondered what leaf this new madness would sprout. So, he told them in plain words. Propelled by the surreal force that had seized him since he set foot into Yanju's desolate room. Possessed beyond reason.

"I'm gay. I knew way before I had sex. Yes, I've had sex. This was why Yanju always took me to church. He wanted to pray it out of me. He wanted to help me with the demons that caused me to self-harm. He knew it would break you two if you ever knew, so he kept my secret. Jealous people will start spreading stories about him now, because he chose to be my friend, but when this happens, this is the truth to believe: he loved me. He loved me like his very own self."

A chill, stilling wave swept through the room. Ini's heart tick-tocked along with the parlour clock.

I can't join you to lie to them anymore.

He had made Yanju proud. He thought of weddings between spirits of the departed and their lovers on earth. He grinned.

His father cleared his throat. "We are going to be late for the funeral, Màmá Inioluwa."

He gently guided his frozen wife outside and locked the door from outside, making sure he turned the key twice.

~

The next morning was a serene Sunday. As Ini hid under his bedsheets, away from his parents' stony, swollen silence, poetry books clumped up around him, he could swear that somebody was singing right outside his window, faintly piercing the still Sunday air, the exact words being:

Light will be the morning

let this dawn sing, sing me a last farewell home.

Home, home to you.

Sweet Basils

CHINONSO NZEH

I.

As the decrepit car totters through the dusty, jagged road in Ekulu, rasping out croaks and crunching gravels, you peek through the window, and a temperate breeze caresses your face.

Things have changed over the last decade in Ekulu, but somehow, everywhere is garbed in the mirage of your childhood. New bungalows have emerged, sitting beside the old ones with peeling paints, draped in bloodless blues and greys. Oby's Bakery, which, in your childhood, was fashioned out of mahogany, is now a large two-story building; that same milky aroma still lingers—you wonder if their milk bread still tastes the same. Memories of when you used to save your lunch money to buy chocolate bread from the bakery after school hours reel in. The area of dense bushes near the rusty signpost that read Ekulu Community School, where Akubueze the madman lived, is now depilated. You wonder where he is. You wonder, too, if his clumpy brown locs have grown longer, if he has lost more teeth, if he has become well, or if, possibly, he has passed away. You remember the times when, as little children, he would chase you all after mocking him. Now, you let out a mild giggle at this memory until your mind veers from the shallow surface to its dingy crypts.

Your breath is revving up. Ripples of hot air spread across your chest, constricting your ribs. In your stomach is a swirling of something tart, an undoing. The image that you loathe and don't want to remember becomes apparent: your father's body at the morgue, swollen and dulled. Cold creeps upon your skin, and, at first, you cannot tell if it is a recollection from the viciously frigid morgue or real cold.

Izunna is talking and chuckling a lot. It piques you, his husky laughter and horrid garrulousness, how he talks to Jideofor, seemingly perfunctory. You want to say shut up and ask what is funny. That doesn't he know that daddy might be dead?

Might.

This startles you: your headstrong use of might, a delusional possibility, a rebellion against reality.

Jideofor senses your irritation and stretches his hands from the passenger's seat beside Izunna who is driving and still talking. He clasps your hands, stroking them with his thumb. You feel a little warmth. His eyes are assuring. They are saying you should pay no mind. You tilt to watch Ijeoma, your two-year-old daughter strapped beside you, sleeping. You keep watching her until the car stops and honks. Until you notice the coppery evening sky. Until you realise you are home.

People are walking out of the family compound, and the few faces you capture are swathed in obligatory grief. As you step out of the car, clutching Ijeoma to your chest, your youngest brothers, Chinonso and Chinedu, both of them twins, standing near the gate and bidding well-wishers goodbye, come to you. They greet you and Jideofor, touching Ijeoma, both of them too excited—amid this despair—to see you. They are grown now, with beards sprouting over their chins, their voices becoming defined baritones, their chests shaping up into the typical masculine build. But you do not tell them these things. You are overpowered by reality. They understand your silence. Izunna beckons them to the boot to take the loads into the house, half-answering some well-wishers. Jideofor takes Ijeoma from you and puts her on his chest. His blue senator outfit billows as he walks beside you.

Trudging into the house with your shades on, you reply to the I am sorrys with a frugal smile and pay no attention to faces even though the voices seem familiar. You want to tell all of them to shut the fuck up, that they should be sorry for themselves, but you get a grip of yourself.

In the quiet of the sitting room is your mother on the slouching beige couch, wrung with terrifying dismay. Her eyes are vacant and weary; her eyebags are sagging so low. She is wielding the air of someone utterly defeated by life. Beside her is Eberechi, Izunna's wife, who is holding her hand and chapping white teeth at you. Stout Eberechi. She stands, adjusting her blue dress to hug you. At first, you try to flinch, but you give in, letting her hug you tightly, inhaling garlic smell.

Aunty Ralu, good afternoon, she says.

You bob your head.

She moves to Jideofor and greets him, patting Ijeoma on her back.

There's a performative manner in how she moves around you, just like her husband does to yours; a forceful pleasing.

You sit beside your mother, unable to say a word. Even though this anguish has stabbed you at your core, you have to be the stronger one. He was her husband, her lover. She knew him first before you did. You hold her hands firmly. A lucid silence swells between you both. The last time you saw her, six months back when she came to your house in Lagos, she was full of life, but now, she's sunk in a chasm. Silent. Her breathing is loud and weighty. Jideofor bends to greet your mother. She takes Ijeoma—who is still asleep—from him, hugs her tightly, glimmers a little, then sighs. She replies to his greeting with an affirming nod. Everyone respects her taciturnity.

Izunna and Eberechi's daughters run out of their room, two of them wearing loose gowns, girls anything from seven to ten. You've never seen them before and cannot remember the exact year they were born. But you remember that the older daughter was born around the time Izunna was rounding up his final year at Enugu State University. Izunna and Eberechi were unmarried then, and, on a thunderous morning, Eberechi's father brought her with a Ghana-Must-Go sack, seething with wrath, threatening to kill Izunna for putting his rubbish seed inside her. It was your father who narrated this story to you with a weary voice over the phone, during your Master's degree program at the University of Lagos. Afterwards, Eberechi would live with your family.

The older daughter has the smile of her mother but a gentle reserve her parents lack. The younger daughter, like Izunna, carries your mother's beautifully rounded face. They greet you and Jideofor, their courtesy well-pronounced but somewhat mechanical, as though Izunna and Eberechi gave them constant lessons. You greet them back, asking how they are and who is who. The older one is Ozioma, the younger one is Chetachi. Ozioma and Chetachi try to hold up Ijeoma from their grandmother, but Eberechi hesitates. She thinks it's better they wait till she's awake.

You would have been spirited if your visit to the village was for another reason. But you cannot feign cheerfulness; your response to each greeting is watery and forced.

Mommy, is this the Aunty Ralu who has plenty of money? Chetachi asks, gawking at you from head to toe.

It's supposed to be a whisper, but everyone hears. Eberechi cups her mouth, fidgeting. An awkward silence follows.

~

It's 1am. You're on the veranda, staring at the flies hovering around the sombre yellow bulb above you. Sleep does not come. You thrust up sighs from time to time. You are numb. Powerless. The image of your father in the mortuary stretches across the walls of your mind. How can? You think. You spoke to him last week on the phone. His voice was frail, but it did not seem like he would die. Or rather, you'd not thought of him dying very recently. How can the father you spoke to a week ago just pass away in his sleep?

You wish it wasn't true. You wish you didn't tell Izunna to take you to the morgue when he picked you and Jideofor at the airport before going home. You wish you didn't walk into that frigid room with pungent smells that almost made you puke.

Now, you want to yell. To pull down things. To rewind. Your chest hurts. Tears refuse to come. You dig your fingers into your skin, clenching your teeth, fuming. Raging at death.

Gone.

You whisper the words repeatedly, putting a higher strain on the next: Gone. GOne. GONE!

Immediately, you drag yourself up from the bench. Your limbs are sore, but you have to. You have to be up by 8am this morning. Your uncles will come for the discussion about your father's burial, as Izunna had said earlier.

2.

The first thing you perceive in your wakefulness is the smell of baby milk, and when you open your eyes, you find Jideofor mixing Ijeoma's milk and cereal inside a small bowl. He is squatting on the floor, mixing them until there are no lumps. Ijeoma, balanced on the seat near him, is beaming and clapping, saying Dada.

I'm with her, Jideofor says. Don't bother. Go and greet mama. Blades of the sun cut through the window, resting on his face. His beard shimmers; his skin glistens.

Ijeoma repeats Mama, stretching her hands toward you, but Jideofor deflects her attention, picking up her iPad from the bed and tuning to Cocomelon.

She'll be fine, he says, blowing you a kiss.

Your eyes have become more aware of this house than they were yesterday. This awareness comes with rage. The rusty roofs, the peeling walls, the broken drainage, the rickety doors.

You burn more when you see the plants in the backyard shrivelling. The Cacti and Snake Plants and Sweet Basils and Garden Crotons and Aloe Vera are turning yellow with uneven hollows on their skin. You touch them— how feeble they have become.

You wonder where the monthly fifty thousand naira for maintaining your father's plants have gone. You wonder where the money for new roofings and paints and drainage has gone. You wonder how all of this is a lie: Izunna crying over the phone, talking about how the wind took out the roofs, how the walls needed plastering and painting, how flood erupted the compound. You remember the many thank you and everything is going fine.

You are angry at the lies, all of them, but the one about the plants disperse something inside you.

At first, your brain slows to a halt. You are baffled and lost. You don't want to make a fuss now. Those godforsaken mourners will be here in no time. You walk back inside, ignoring Eberechi's hysterical greeting, Chinedu's what should I do for you, and Chinonso's did you sleep well? You walk into your father's room, knowing your madness will bare itself if something is in chaos here.

But nothing is. Your mother is on the bed, eating oats. Each morsel she downs is a struggle.

You sit with her, and you remember the times you sat on this bed with her while she braided your hair into cornrows on Sunday evenings in your childhood, as the smell of Damatol and jelly oil dawdled in the air. You remember the intimate moments with your mother: both of you bonding over food, or the latest village gossip, or the men who chased you.

Mummy, are you okay? You ask.

She sighs and says, they said I should eat so that I won't slump and die. My husband anwụọla just like that. She heaves another sigh, this one carrying more weight than the first. She stops eating. You clasp her hands, and your eyes catch a portrait of your father in his youth hung near the wardrobe: wearing a hat, grinning, arms akimbo.

You do not notice when Chinedu walks in. But now he's standing beside your father's empty clay flower pot. His eyes are red, and he's holding a napkin. You wish you could console him and Chinonso; they, too, need solace. It's been a long time since you sat with them, these twin brothers who will become university graduates soon.

Uncle Eloka and the other elders are outside. I was cleaning the chairs when they came. They want to do the meeting already.

You stand up and ask, Do we have anything to offer them? Like malt? Garden eggs? Kolanuts? Anything at all? We have to give them something. You know these people and their wahala.

Chinedu bobs his head in affirmation. Brother Izunna bought a few things yesterday. But we haven't bought anything for the mourners yet.

Why the hell do we have to buy anything for mourners? Your voice is terse and rutted.

He doesn't reply.

Stay with Mama, let me go and meet the elders. Where's Nonso?

I think he's at the gate, waiting to welcome today's visitors. Like people from Mama's church and all.

Oh.

You walk out.

At the front of your veranda, six men in red caps and Isiagu clothing occupy the white plastic chairs, one of whom is your Uncle Eloka. He's still the same—round body, guileful smile, uncontained air. He stands up to hug you, his walking stick an aid, and he has stooped from old age.

Ada daddy! How are you? You're a big woman, oh! His face is glowing with excitement, but a mild irritation flares up in you when you remember that this same Uncle Eloka verbally wrestled your father for sending you to the university instead of marrying you off. You had aced your Senior School Certificate Examinations and your matriculation exams, set to get into the University of Lagos. One Sunday evening, he came to visit, and your father handed him your result slips in exhilaration while he ate the native jollof rice your mother cooked. He stared at the papers for a while, squinting.

She's going to University for what now? Do you want her to decay? Let her marry! See Ugorji's daughter. She's married to Ezeka's son who has money. These things will corrupt this girl. At least, you can send Izunna and the twins. They are boys! He had said.

Your father took the papers back, startled. My daughter will go to university, he had fired back, his tone a flat metre, an assurance and a declaration.

I am doing well, Uncle, you say to him.

Oh, nne'm! My brother's death is sad. We cannot even tell how he just went like that in his sleep. But, you know, our people say it's a good death. He's surely resting well. He tilts his lips downwards.

Ndo, nne. It is the albino man with the freckles-strewn face beside Uncle Eloka. Take heart. Udeh was a kind-hearted man, and now that he's dead, he deserves a befitting burial, so we want to plan well.

You sit on the wooden bench placed adjacent to them.

Eberechi walks in with a stool and a plate filled with kola nuts and menthol candy, greets the men, and places the stool in the middle where they can all reach for the kola nuts and menthol.

How do we begin? You ask.

They stare at each other, muddied, all four of them. They are mumbling.

Where is Izunna and your husband, Jideofor?

My husband is feeding my daughter, Ijeoma. He should be here soon. I'm not sure about Izunna. I think he went to buy fuel. He should be here soon, too.

Your husband is feeding your daughter? Uncle Eloka laughs and faces the freckled-face albino elder beside him and the rest of the men. Doesn't your husband have a penis? How can he be feeding your daughter and you're here with us in the meeting—a place for nwoke? Your husband is family now, so he should be here.

You are taken aback. Heat surges within you. Does this bastard uncle think I'm the Ralu that would keep her mouth shut whenever someone said bullshit to her face? You think. You want to tell him to shut up. To get out of this house. That you can handle your father's burial without all of them. Afterall, you are the one handling the expenses for the funeral. You want to scream. Your eyes are scalding. You are weak in the face of everything, but crying right in front of these men will leave you defeated. Jideofor comes out, wearing brown corduroy pants and a white polo that hugs him so tightly and shows his ripped chest. His face is straight as he greets the elders. They greet him back, dousing their sense of intimidation with hard smiles.

I heard them, Jideofor says, his voice a little lower than a whisper. Pay them no mind. It's just this week only—we can compromise with their bleakness. I left Ijeoma with her cousin sisters, and they were so happy to see her. They are playing with her.

You sigh, stand up, and, as you're about to leave, Uncle Eloka asks if you don't want to stay with Jideofor. You ignore him, and he is silent, perhaps because Jideofor is here.

In the hallway, Eberechi stops you to say something, but, as politely as you can muster, you tell her to excuse you. You don't like her eagerness to be in close contact with you.

3.

It's been an hour and thirty minutes since the meeting started. You wonder what Uncle Eloka is saying—the conversation he and the other elders deem you unfit to be part of. You try to swerve your mind off it, but it dwells. You've been sitting on the bed in this room that was once yours and is now a guest room, looking at the walls in sweeping silence. This room where, as a young girl, you sat on this bed, a stool before you, with books strewn around, studying hard for your senior school certificate exams, dreaming you would become a lecturer. And now, years later, on this same bed, you open your laptop and go through the Gmail notifications you made a mental note to revisit yesterday. Tons of sorry and rest in peace and take hearts from your students at the sophisticated private University in Lagos, where you teach philosophy. You ignore the emails. The more you read them, the more your spirit sags.

You think of this dream that your father held to. You remember how you wrote boldly in your matriculation form: University of Lagos as your school of choice and Philosophy as your preferred course. You remember how much you read, denying yourself of sleep, your father often staying awake with you to make sure you covered topics, even though he didn't fully understand how these things worked because he was illiterate. You remember how he paid your first school fees and left you wondering how he got such money, only to find out that he sold his bike, a possession that had been dear to his heart. You remember how your mother begged him to repeal the idea of sending you to the university, not because she didn't want you there, but because she was enormously saturated in twirling to the whims of Umunna, frightened by what they would say. You remember how your father rebuked her.

You are washed with mild satisfaction and excruciating twinges, the former because your father watched you graduate, run your master's degree, and your doctorate program. But excruciating twinges because he could have seen more, because you rarely spent time with him in the recent times before he died, except when he visited—which was very rarely—your house in Lagos, because now, you're no longer sure if he received the gifts and money you sent to him through Izunna.

Your phone rings. You hesitate before you check who it is.

Jude. Your housekeeper in Lagos.

You pick up the call.

Hello madam, his voice is sudsy in a way you don't like.

It takes you almost a minute before you say hello. All through yesterday and today, you'd forgotten about your home in Lagos.

Jude, how are you?

Madam, I dey all right. I bin call because you never call me since yesterday morning when you and Oga take flight go village.

Oh. Thank you for reaching out. How are my plants?

Ah, all of them dey well oh. I dey take care of them like say na children them be.

They are children. They are my children. I hope you didn't dispose of that sweet basil. Did you?

His silence nearly suffocates you.

Did you throw it away? You tense up.

No oh. God forbid. Why I go throway am? I just keep am one side dey nurture am, although no progress.

Keep watering it, and send me the picture on WhatsApp, and keep the house clean. Am I clear?

Yes, madam.

Okay. Be calling. From time to time.

Bye, ma.

~

Three days ago, after you came back from lecturing your students, you met your favourite plant, Sweet Basil—the one with the rounded and curved sides and reddish body your father had taught you how to plant as a child— withering. You were dazed. This plant was often met with the sun, it consumed water, and fed on rich manure. Now, it has shrunken. You called Jude and Ijeoma's nanny, screaming at them for being present in the slow cessation of the plant.

Jideofor came home, which was way earlier than usual on a Tuesday afternoon. You had your lectures up till 1 p.m. on Tuesday. He, a lecturer in the Economics department, had his up to 4. From his face, you could tell that something was wrong. You asked him, and he kept faltering, the words too hard to fall out of his mouth. Did he have an issue with his students at school?

They said that Papa is dead, he said after so much persuasion, stuttering. Something in you died.

~

Even though you're not superstitious, today, you try to defy your logic. What if the plant was Papa's way of saying goodbye? You think. After all, you've heard stories like this one. You remember the story of the woman whose chandelier fell from her ceiling and broke, and hours later, she heard the news of her husband dead in a fatal accident.

When you were younger, your father grew plants on Saturday evenings after he took a leave from his security guard job at Polaris Bank near Saint Peter's Primary School. In the small space in your backyard, he grew beautiful plants—Aloe Vera, Ixora, Garden Crotons, Cacti, Snake Plants, and his favourite, Sweet Basil. He did not call it Sweet Basil. Aside from Aloe Vera, he had random names for them because he did not know their real names. Like Ixora, he called it Ifuru Kpakpando. He called the Cacti Chuku-Chuku. He called the Snake Plants Osisi Agwo. He called the Garden Crotons Nnukwu Osisi. And he called the Sweet Basil, his favourite, Egwurugwuru Osisi. He liked how the plants looked, how colourful they were, and because he liked them, you began to like them, too. He said there was something about the colours and the simplicity.

You were the only child of his who liked growing flowers with him on Saturday evenings. You would watch him at first, then you learned how to grow them too, and then you developed an intense love like his. Your father stopped growing flowers while you were in the university, and when you came home for the holidays, you asked him, and he said, No one wants to plant with me. I cannot do it alone. I need someone who loves this thing like me, and you're in University.

You made sure to send money out of the little you earned at the printing shop in school to take care of the plants. And when you were home, you made sure to actively grow plants with him. Years later, you would own different plants in your house in Lagos, especially the Sweet Basil plants.

Last week, he talked about Sweet Basils, saying he needed more for the compound whenever you were coming to Ekulu.

Your anger for Izunna is ignited again as you think of the hungering flowers in the backyard.

4.

Outside, crickets are creaking, overrunning the stark quiet of the night. Your body starts to rave, surges of desire crushing you. You stare at Jideofor, who is sleeping. You tap him. Twice. He wakes up, scratching his eyes with the back of his palm.

What's wrong? He asks, his voice torpid.

Let's make love, you say, grazing the arcs of his chest.

Are you sure? Are you all right? But Ijeoma? He stares at you under the pale light, gaining full consciousness.

Yes, you say, shifting Ijeoma to the other side of the bed, demarcating the space with the green duvet.

You reach for his crotch, tickling it, and, still unsure as though not to harm you, he meets your lips, carefully fondling your breasts as you let out very quiet moans because of Ijeoma. He trails your body with kisses, and then he thrusts, reiterating sessions of exhilaration, slow and fast, until you both reach the apex.

He lays his weight on your body, pressing your breasts flat, nuzzling you. You want him to stay like this all night, on you. You are amazed—how this desire spins so angrily in your time of anguish.

You feel a certain kind of gratitude to Jideofor. You're not certain if you should feel or cast off this feeling about someone who has become your home.

It's been eight years since you met him at the genteel university where you teach philosophy in Lagos. It was one of your first months as a lecturer. You were invited to speak at a symposium on Lecturers' Day as one of the youngest lecturers in the school. The curator, Professor Charles Akwen, had told you that there was also another young person who would speak. You were curious to know who this was. After you spoke, a young man with a ball of afro—now, he's on a low cut—wearing a blue kaftan emerged on stage. There was a winsome disposition added to the way he was; his baritone was clear as water, and he held up a confidence that wasn't snazzy. A confidence that spoke for itself.

You did not stop thinking about him. Eventually, you would bump into each other at the research library near the faculty of arts. Surprisingly, he said hi first and asked what you were doing at the research library even though he knew. The next week, you both went on a date at a restaurant in Victoria

Island. That same week, you both went to the arts theatre at the faculty of arts to see a play. Your love for each other glid so effortlessly. You shared many of the same things: doting on flowers, reading books on world history, Asa's music, Egusi soup, Arundhati Roy, SDG 5, and your agnosticism. The week after, you were in his house, curled beside him, naked. The month after that, he was in yours. The year after that, both of you were sharing vows on the altar at the cathedral in Lagos Island, with your family and his, all dressed in dazzling laces, chanting Amen to each vow you made.

~

You stare at each other until you fall asleep.

5.

Izunna honks from outside, a scratching honk, and it ricochets into the house, across the walls. From your room, wearing a pink boubou, you hear Izunna say, Ralu, time is going, please, be fast. The Reverend father will leave soon. You want to say, Don't rush me, you fraud. But you say nothing. You are quiet now, your bangles are clinking, and Jideofor is watching you as he dusts off his sandals.

Inside the car, as Izunna drives through the bumpy road, you want to question him. To ask why he misappropriated the money you sent him for your parents and the house. You want to slap him. To tell him to stop the car already. But you keep calm; you want to be done with everything. You think of the times in your childhood when you bristled with him, when you both argued over a piece of meat, when he called you nkita, when he pulled your mgbeke wig at the amusement park in Agbani. Mischievous and intelligent Izunna, who, now, has become someone you don't fully know. This Izunna who is four years younger than you. Izunna who was at the top of his class, became the head boy in secondary school, was the best in his year's matriculation examination; now Izunna who worked at a Merchant

Bank in Udi and was later sacked for multiple fabrications. Izunna who used Chinonso and Chinedu's university registration fees to play gamble.

Today, he's not saying anything; he's not laughing. Maybe he now knows that nothing is funny. You think of Ijeoma, how she's faring without you or Jideofor. You try to yank your mind off her, but you cannot.

Saint Stephen's Catholic Church hasn't changed, except for the faultlessly pruned flower beds that have grown larger, and the towering palm trees that no longer stand beside the statue of the Virgin Mary holding a rosary. You wonder where they are now. As you walk into the reverend father's office, closely behind Izunna and beside Jideofor, a woody smell fills your nose and rushes to your throat, reminding you of confessions on Saturdays. You remember how you came to the then Reverend father, broken and with a contrite heart, to confess your sins—how you kissed Obioma, your classmate in secondary school; how you stole mangoes from Mazi Okoro's compound; how you muttered Akwunakwuna when Mrs. Cherechi the English teacher who wore a frown too often flogged you eight strokes of cane because you had an incomplete note.

This new reverend father is young, nothing like the one you knew who was old and had cynical eyes, maybe your age mate, thirty-seven or so. He urges you three to take your seats in the name of the Lord and, as you all do, he says Hail Mary and observes silence for your father, and you let Izunna speak because you no longer know how to associate with faith talks, even though, now, it involves your father. All you do is nod, say yes, no, and I think so.

After all is said and done, and lists are given to you, you tell Izunna and Jideofor to leave you, that you will come back home with a tricycle, and that you want to spend time in the church. You want to feel your father. Izunna takes heed, but Jideofor is taken aback.

What do you want to do inside a church? He says, flushing with sarcasm.

His question aggravates you. Yes, you no longer associate with the faith, but who is he to question how you want to mourn your father? You do not reply to him, and he notices the anger on your face and tries to apologise with his eyes, but you ignore him. Instead, you walk into the large church and sit on the pew in the first row.

You are staring at the image of Jesus Christ on the cross hung near the altar. You don't know: should you pray or just sit in silence? You want to feel something, anything. In your mind's eye, your father is beside you, smiling and nodding to the soft symphony of the choir singing Rock of Ages.

You lost your faith nearly a decade ago during your master's program at the University of Lagos. You cannot trace the exact it happened, but you remember swerving to your subconscious, succumbing to this truth you had known but were scared to acknowledge.

You did not tell your father about this loss. You feared he would rebuke you. Your father, a solemn catholic, who donned his faith so firmly. You also did not tell him that Jideofor, your suitor at the time, was irreligious. Both of you had planned a religious wedding to please your parents—Jideofor's parents, too, were strong and, in his words, "sometimes polemic Pentecostals," and he was nothing.

When you finally told your mother two years ago when she came to Lagos for Ijeoma's omugwo, she told your father. She never mentioned that she did, but you noticed from the many Have you prayed the rosary today? Do you still recite novenas? and I pray the grace of the Virgin Mary is brimming over and changes your heart that your father sent you. Even when he came to visit, he never spoke about it.

Now, even though you do not believe anymore, you sit in silence, hear the large clock chime, and observe the melancholia on the portrait of Jesus Christ on the altar.

I was worried for you, your mother says, sitting on the bench on the veranda, holding a lamp, her face creased in unease. They just took the light. They said you went to church. I was happy, but I began to fear when you took so much time. I was now thinking, do they want to take my Ralu away from me, too? Her voice was bland; her face was straight.

Oh, no, mama. I'm okay. I'm well. Nothing's wrong.

You check your phone for the time, and the bright light flickers on your face. 10:43 pm.

Mommy, aren't you supposed to be sleeping? And why didn't Nedu or Nonso put on the generator? It'll be hot, and Ijeoma won't even sleep without a fan or air conditioner. I'm particularly worried for her.

I cannot sleep, and your husband was about to give Nonso money for fuel but the fuel stations have closed.

You say nothing. You are happy she's a little responsive. Oya mommy, let's go and sleep. I want to sleep with you today. Jideofor will do well with Ijeoma.

Ah, are you sure? You know men cannot take care of—

No, mama. Not like that with us.

You take the lamp for her and let her go first, then you shut the door.

6.

Today, you are startled at your slowness in adaptation. At first, when you wake up, you want to ask your father at the veranda where he kept the watering can. And as you reach the veranda, there is no father there; reality dawns on you.

You are planting and pruning. Nearly all the flowers are shrivelling, but you try. You carefully pluck out the bad ones, arrange the fairly good ones, and moisturise them, replenishing the soils, too. The Sweet Basils are part of the fairly good ones, even though hollows appear on their pale skin. This gladdens your spirit: that the plant your father adored so terribly is one of the plants alive. You think of Izunna, the things you'll say to him after the burial, the outpour of anger you've been squelching beneath as respect for your father. After the burial, your uproar will unravel itself upon Izunna.

Still pruning and planting, you think of names as a collective tradition. Your father was the only one who called you Afunwaelotanna. These plants bear w itness to that naming. You were fourteen when he first called you that name. You got into an accident on a bus when you went to buy wheat flour at Ekegbo market which was nearly thirty-five minutes away from your house, and amid your pain and before you blanked out, you wondered how your parents would locate you there.

You found yourself in a hospital bed surrounded by a few people, their faces too hard to recognize. Then came your father and mother rambling in fear. Your father was quiet, in shock, and your mother was shrieking. A week after, while you both were tending to the plants, your father said that some people recognized you because they were sure he was your father; the resemblance was explicit. And he began to call you Afunwaelotanna—I've seen the child and I remember the father.

This reality is one of the things you cannot fully embrace; that the name has served its purpose and will forever be buried with your father.

7.

The priest in the ballooning cassock is saying a prayer. A siren is wailing. Cries, muffled and loud, fill the air. Your father's casket is in front of you. Near the plants in the compound. A brown casket emblazoned with gold flanks. Everyone in the family is wearing white lace, including your uncles and their wives with deadpan faces. Your mother and Chinedu and Chinonso and Eberechi and Izunna are beside you, crying. Your mother's cry is hushed, but her eyes are a roaring red. Chinedu's wailing is mixed with a series of brief breaths. Chinonso's cry is from within—a quelled whimper. Eberechi's cry is so loud that you want to gatekeep her mourning. Izunna is not crying. He is wearing a semblance of resilience; sorrow is veiled under it. Jideofor is behind you, holding your waist, and, like you, he's wearing sunshades. Ijeoma and her cousins are inside the house, shut from the rest of the world, maybe watching Barbie or playing with Ijeoma's dolls. Jideofor brought the suggestion; he thought the event too traumatising for kids.

His casket is open now. For the last time. Four able-bodied men stand beside it. You catch a glimpse of his body arrayed in a white suit, hands gloved, feet covered with white stockings, and a rosary around his neck. You take your eyes off. Jideofor holds you tightly, patting your back. And this is the first time you weep, hyperventilating intensely, profusely.

You are the first person the priest calls upon to throw dust into the ground your father lay. As you pick up a shovel and throw dust, your hand trembles. You tell Jideofor to take you back inside the house. You cannot take all of this and cannot stay till the end. No one questions you.

Inside the sitting room, Ijeoma and her cousins are crouched together on the slouching beige sofa, watching television. Your phone rings so loudly from the room. Jideofor tells you to stay right there, that he'll get it for you.

It's Jude. You're wondering why he's calling.

Ehen? What happened? Didn't I mention that my father's burial is today? I said no calls.

Ah, madam, No vex. I don forget, I swear. Sorry for your loss once again. I call you to tell you say that flower, sweet basin abi wetin you dey call am, e don dey heal. The body don come outside and the colour don dey show small-small.

Your hands quiver till your phone falls off. You feel flappings inside your belly, a lightness in your being. Jideofor asks what is wrong, but you cannot will your lips to move.

And you are crying all over again.

Yesterday and Today and Tomorrow 🄴
MUSTAPHA ENESI

Here is a woman whose life is bereft of happiness. She sits on a wooden armchair crafted specially for her, built by the furniture man who lives just across her house; an armchair with wheels and rims and tubeless tires, made specially for her condition—'Alzheimer's,' the doctors called it. She sits on her wooden armchair as if alone, in her tiny two-bedroom apartment, staring and staring out the window. But she is not alone. And she is not complete. Not that she has ever been complete or has ever lived a life with any sense of completeness. Her youthfulness has been snatched by the ugly nature of life itself, completely disregarding her body in all its glory. Her full lips, high cheekbones, her skin the colour of brown clay, full black and curly hair, curvy body, long eyelashes, and all the things that make women so pretty, one can tell by a mere glance.

She now cannot conceive of her husband, also in old age, who sits by her all day and night, waiting for when she will snap out of *it*. Waiting for when she will look away from the window, turn her head to him and say smiling, "Greg, you are here?" in that way that makes happiness creep up her face and disappear, just about the time he tries to smile back and reply. Three times daily, she snaps out of *it*. She cannot conceive of her husband who she has never believed looked one bit like her. When friends and family and acquaintances and strangers they encountered at the market stole glances from her face to her husband's face, and from her husband's face to her face, and declared that they looked alike; that married couples always looked alike. And now, they actually look alike—both with wrinkled skin, grey hairs, and droopy, unhappy eyes—but she cannot conceive of him.

She cannot conceive of their dying love; or of yesterday and today and tomorrow; or of how day followed night and rainy season followed dry season; or of how lunch followed breakfast; or the seemingly endless cycle they exist in; or the nature and the purpose and the end that will come out of their marriage. She cannot conceive of the wind that blows dust to her face, or the smell of something nostalgic hitting her nose—ginger, a lost baby, a misplaced career. She cannot conceive of anything remotely reminding her of Sundays—the jingle of church bells, the baritone texture of the pastor screaming into the microphone, the harmonious seraphic voices, the soothing nature of praise and worship, and the essence of community. She cannot conceive of Bosede, her house-help who had one day, a long time ago, run into her compound dragging her mounds of problems with her—debts and bills and a hungry stomach—asking for a job, "I dey wash clothes pass machine madam," she'd said.

Bosede, who prepares her daily ginger tea mixed with honey. Bosede, who started moving around the house with that peppery hot smell of ginger stamped on her body since her madam's diagnosis. And here sits her madam in her armchair, staring at nothing. At nothing. At nothing!

When she turns her face from the window, her husband is standing by the dining table. He looks washed and clean, in freshly laundered clothes prepared for him by Bosede. He smells of lavender. He sits down on one of the chairs at the dining table, and with his own hands, by his own strength, makes himself a sandwich: two slices of bread, one boiled egg, two slices of cheese, and one hot cup of beverage. He eats. He hears everything at once; the mooing of cows in the distance, the barking of a dog, the clucking of a hen, all crescendoing. Walking over, the woman places her hands on his shoulders, caressing the small of his back. And her husband, sipping his hot cup of beverage, wanting to stand up to kiss her—on the lips if she had snapped out of *it,* and on the forehead if she hadn't.

"Gregory," she says, pausing as if to collect her thoughts. "Our son will be home today, did you know? He is coming, did you know?"

And by this, he knows that she hasn't snapped out of *it.*

The man stops eating, he stops drinking. He stands up and holds his wife. He looks and looks at her with pity, and he is in pain, and she looks back at him, her face flushed with confusion. *And who is this man?* She wonders— vacant brown eyes with a pain she does not understand. What is this goodness in him? And why does it now matter? Why is she suddenly remembering a time, not too long ago, when she was with child? Three times she had been pregnant.

The first time it happened, she was sixteen. Her cousin, Bolu or Tolu or whatever his name was had made her pregnant, and by force, tearing into her, muffling her screams. Her mother had wrapped her complaints into loud hisses and tossed them aside. And so she had taken matters into her own hands, eating and drinking and swallowing all the things she had learned could help get rid of unwanted *things* by the people who knew how well to get rid of unwanted *things*.

The second time she took in, she was twenty-three. She was a young adult, jumping from one party to another, from one man to another, and from one hangover to another. She tried to get rid of it, too. From all she'd learned from the people who knew how to get rid of unwanted *things*. But all the things she knew—all the concoctions and pills and lying flat on the stomach—did not work. She gave birth, one midnight, alone, under the Student Union mounted canopy, near one of the university's lecture theatres. All bloodied, both baby and mother. At the break of dawn, she abandoned the baby, in a carton, at a dump, near an orphanage.

The third time, by the time she was married to Gregory, the baby had died in her sleep. She never loved Gregory. She never wanted to marry him. So, when the doctors told her the baby had choked on breastmilk, she cut her hair and cried herself to bed. Afterwards, she began to seek out life itself, waiting for the better days to come. Walking around the house, all gloomy, all sad. Lifted up by celebrations: Christmas dinners, New Year, thanksgiving, wedding bells of newlywed couples at the church. Weighed down by the loneliness and terror that engulfed her and her husband. Where were these days? These fleeting non-existent days. The days never came. Because had they come, her house would have been full of mispronounced words, gibberish, the smell of puke and fresh diapers and baby oil and powder. There would have been children crossing the road on their way to school and returning home with dirty uniforms. There would have been laughter, uncontrolled laughter, sibling rivalry, abundant energy, and endless homework. Just last month—before the diagnosis, before the shifting of time and memory—she had wanted a divorce.

Gregory leads her back to her armchair, and she sits. On one hand, she has experienced life; all-night parties, flashing lights, clicking heels, and great sex. But she also feels emptiness and yearning for unfulfilled desires. Her husband feels hope and love and faith and healing. He kisses her on the forehead and she doesn't respond. Not even a shudder. Not even a blink. Not a single recognition. Sitting in front of him, on the armchair with wheels and rims and tubeless tires is indeed his wife, a vast shell of dreadful silence. But the woman does not notice.

Right there, on the armchair, she reimagines her life. She will be with child, again. A fourth pregnancy. A boy. A baby boy. And she will name him Sam. The naming ceremony will be talked about for days. But the baby will come out in 7 months instead of the full 9, feeble and weak. The doctors will tell her to bathe Sam with caution, to simply dab his body with a damp towel for one full month, at least. To not shake the baby. Sam will suckle and suckle and suckle till his mother looks malnourished. And Gregory's mother will come and she will bathe Sam and she will shake him and shake him and shake him. The woman will make him drink àgbo. And in the morning, Sam's body will be stiff and blue. He will be dead. She will cry and cry and lose her voice, and she will tell Gregory's mother to leave her house, threatening to arrest her with the police, calling her a ruthless witch.

She reimagines her life with another child—her fifth pregnancy. Gregory will be useless. He will drink and smoke and his eyes will always be red. He will beat her on days the breakfast is too cold, and stifle a frown on his face when dinner is too light. And one day, she will be 6 months gone and too tired to cook anything. There will be no Bosede to help. And Gregory will stagger in at midnight, a stench of alcohol oozing from his body, meeting no food, no cold or light dinner on the table. He will get angry and roar and rush into their room and kick her, on the head; kick her, on her legs; kick her, on her bulging stomach. He will kick her everywhere. He will kick her till her foetus, a baby girl the size of a kitten, drops from her legs. Bloodied, fully formed, dead. And the week after while at work, Gregory will die from the sting of a bee. The sting will be in anger and fright, pricked into the corner of his mouth. He will die. She will be a widow.

She reimagines her life, this time without a child. No miscarriages. No stillbirths. No drinking Gregory. This time, Bosede is sleeping with Gregory, and though they try to hide it, she knows. She knows of the different times her husband has emptied himself inside Bosede's body. A quickie in the bathroom; hours of fucking, long into the dead of the night, with muffled moans in the living room when they think she is deeply asleep. When the morning sickness starts, she knows Bosede will give birth to twins. At last, her house will be full of mispronounced words, and gibberish, and the smell of puke, and the smell of fresh diapers, and the smell of baby oil and baby powder. There will be children crossing the road on their way to school. There will be children returning home from school with dirty uniforms. There will be laughter, uncontrolled laughter, sibling rivalry, abundant energy, and endless homework. And it didn't matter if they were not her own children. But Bosede will run away with the twins and there will be none of these. She will be alone, again, with this husband she never loved.

Now, she summons up her children. And she can see, from simply staring out the window, all three of them. Briefly they appear, shrouded in fear and abandonment and neglect. Like they had emerged from burning coal, chipped, in fragments, unloved. There is a grey hue around them, like they had been in and out of water. Wet and dry and dry and wet. Hot and cold and cold and hot. These children whom she would have loved better than her house and her money and her husband and her beauty. These children who would have been beautiful boys and girl. These children would have been named Sam, Micheal, and Rose.

"Mother, why do you look so afraid? Why don't you come and join us, eh?" Sam says to her.

She has no answer. Her children, Sam, Micheal, and Rose, all three of them, laugh at her. She shudders, feeling mocked, shaking her head, whispering, "No, no, no." Then the wind blows to her face from the window, and she doesn't smell dust or ginger. She smells death.

Dead now are her children. Dead now is yesterday and today, and dead shall tomorrow be. Dead is the day that follows night and the rainy season that follows the dry season, and the lunch that follows breakfast. And who stands behind her, this husband of hers, as soon as she snaps out of *it,* dead too shall their marriage be.

Just as they appeared, her children, they vanished. Everything has its season. Time has never been more fleeting and fragile. Time has never been kind to her. Nothing has ever been kind to her.

She remembers her childhood, bereft of love. How unwanted she had felt. How she had struggled to teach herself to love herself. How she had struggled to make her mother love her. How her mother punished her for the littlest things. Once when her mother caught her masturbating, the woman had cut lines on her fingers with a razor and rubbed habanero pepper into the cuts. No kind scolding. No loving hatred. No motherly contempt.

Her mother never taught her how to thread a needle or sew a patch on a worn-out dress. Her mother never taught her how to sit like a woman, or in what way to talk to boys. Her mother never taught her how to pick pumpkin leaves or how to cook them. Her mother never taught her how to not disgrace the family or how to keep good friends. Her mother never taught her how to deal with boys who harass her. Her mother never taught her love and happiness and kindness and the many other things that make a daughter a daughter. Her mother never told her about miscarriages and stillbirths and how to carry herself after the sudden death of a newborn child. Her mother never taught her how to marry a man she was not in love with. And her mother never taught her how to say, *Back to sender,* snapping her fingers in circular movements around her head to people who had snapped their fingers at her over a heated disagreement. She would have been different. She would have taught her daughter many things. She would have loved her daughter so dearly. She would have been a good mother.

Now in her room, she stands in front of a mirror. And she sees her skin, shrouded in fear and abandonment and neglect. She is pale. Very pale. No full lips. No high cheekbones. No full black and curly hair. No curvy body, and no long eyelashes. She doesn't feel like the self she had once known. She feels giddy like she is no longer made of blood and flesh. No muscles, no life to look forward to. She remembers that there is a name for the thing she has, but she doesn't remember what it is called. She has no name for the thing she is now, and she knows it is not simply old age. She feels like a window, an open space from which she lets light and wind and children through. Light that comes after dark. Wind that comes after stillness. Children that come after childlessness. And she sees, for the first time in a long time, that she is beautiful—despite her wrinkled skin, grey hairs, and droopy, unhappy eyes, she is still beautiful. This beauty is not like that of a newborn baby's smile or the spreading of a peacock's feathers. This beauty is of old age, of vibrant wrinkles and skinfolds.

She goes back to sitting in the armchair with wheels and rims and tubeless tires, built by the furniture man who lives just across her house; built for her condition. And she stares and stares out the window. Her husband, Gregory, stands behind her, pressing his hands gently into the small of her back, humming, singing Onyeka Onwenu's "You and I Will Live as One". There, they are one and the same and the same and one. He presses his feeble, old hands into the small of her back till they are indistinguishable. Man and woman. Husband and wife. Father and Mother of dead Sam. And this way they are in love, Gregory thinks. And he, once again, feels hope and faith and light and healing, and he bends to place a kiss on her forehead. But she turns abruptly, and she pushes him away, screaming and ululating.

"Stop! Tolu, please, stop! Please! Don't do this!"

She stops, her face going blank. Tears rolling down her eyes. She goes back to staring at the window, and there is wind blowing at her face, and she smells dust, and she smells ginger, and she hears the groaning of Gregory and the quick footsteps of Bosede, and she hears all the mooing and the barking and the clucking, and she sees her children once again—Sam, and Micheal, and Rose—and she smiles, and tries to spread her arms, and tries to reach for them, but she feels herself grow solid, stiffening, happiness filling her mouth, and she shuts her eyes, feeling complete at last.

Choice, not Feeling

OBINNA INOGBO

"Can you dress sexier?" Dare asks, staring ahead at the smart TV without looking at her.

Kemi winces. Her sundress is crowned with a bolero. They're in his Sangotedo living room. Dare's legs are stretched on the velvet L-shaped sofa. She's seated next to him, her legs planted in wedges on the marble-tiled floor. The standing rechargeable fan whirs. ESPN Sportscenter is on.

"You don't like the way I look?" she asks.

He sighs. "You could look better," he replies. "I mean, you have a nice body, I don't know why you're always hiding it."

Tears well up in her eyes. She looks away from him, opening her bag to fetch a tissue. He's still watching Sportscenter. "You know I'm not busty and I'm very self-conscious about it."

"So, what? They're millions of women all over Lagos with small breasts who take pride in them."

She looks at him. "Where's this coming from?"

He sighs. "Yomi had a house party on Friday and all the guys were there with their women. The women were sexy, and I was there alone because I didn't want to take you."

"Why didn't you want to take me?"

He looks at her for a second before returning his gaze to the TV. "Because I knew you'd stand out by looking unsexy."

"Wow! So, you have such little faith in me! Have you ever invited me to a party before? Why didn't you wait and see whether I would surprise you?" She stands up. "And by the way, it's not everything about you I like! What kind of businessman sits at home all day watching TV? Even if you already have customers, can't you go out and look for more?"

"Then why are you still here?"

She makes a beeline for the door, slamming it shut as she leaves. She re-enters almost immediately, struts to his fridge, removes a big Tupperware of okra soup and walks out of the flat, leaving the door open.

~

"She took the soup she made for you?" Tayo laughs. His date laughs as well. Seated on his laps, she's in her mid-twenties, wearing a playsuit and nude clear strap open-toe heels. Tayo caresses her thigh with one hand, while he holds his drink in the other hand. His short-sleeved button-up shirt has the top two buttons undone.

"And that soup sweet, die," Dare replies. "Remember the ẹfọ́ríró she made for my thirty-fifth birthday last year? I'll give it to her sha. She cooks well, tidies up my place, makes sure there are diffusers in every room—"

"Why did you let her go then?" Tayo's date asks. "I won't even do any of that for Tayo unless he marries me."

"Dare, can you see how I'm suffering?" Tayo says, looking at Dare.

The Afrobeats music is loud, but the lounge patrons can still hear each other in a conversation. There are fifty people present in the dimly lit, air-conditioned environment. Five waiters are on serving duty, walking in and out of the main lounge and behind the circular long bar.

Tayo's date munches on a spring roll as she scrolls through her phone. "Do you like this my friend?" she asks Dare, showing him her phone. Dare looks at the twenty-something dark-skinned lady in an above-the-knee fitted LBD.

"Mandy. Where's she from?" he asks her.

"Port Harcourt. She's an influencer."

"Yeah? Which brands?"

"When you see her ask her!"

Dare smiles. He picks up his phone and opens Instagram. "I've followed her. Give me her number."

Tayo smiles. "Back in the streets already!"

"No time, bro," Dare replies.

Tayo's date signals to the waiter. Tayo shakes his head at Dare. "This one won't kill me. Na so-so cocktail she dey order."

"Shebi you just collected salary this morning? Let's spend it na!" Tayo's date says.

Dare laughs. Tayo shakes his head again.

~

"I did my ass and boobs last year," Mandy says, looking at Dare as she twirls the straw in her cocktail. Dare notices a mole at the top of her left breast. She's wearing an off-shoulder dress with gladiator sandals. Wafts of cigarette smoke filter around them.

"Oh...okay," he replies, taking off his sunglasses.

"What? Why are you shocked? All your faves do it."

He signals to the waiter and asks for more ketchup.

"Tayo says you're doing well," she says, breaking the crab with her fingers. "Some kind of app?"

"You know Tayo?" he asks, spreading ketchup over his fries.

"Of course. My friend carries him on top her head."

He laughs. "Why won't she? Tayo has been balling since we finished youth service."

"So, what do you have planned for me today?"

His eyebrows narrow. "Er, we're here having brunch, I thought—"

"No ooo. You're taking me out for the whole day. This date doesn't finish 'til midnight. Tomorrow morning, if you act right."

He smiles. "So, how's influencing?"

"I'm three years in. It could be better. I'm not satisfied."

"But the boob job and BBL?"

"You're getting too personal."

"Sorry."

"I'm joking," she laughs. "You're too serious! We need to loosen you up!" She signals the waiter. "Can we have tequila shots?" she asks the young man. He nods, scribbling on a small notepad before scurrying off to the bar.

"I did a huge football job last year: that's what paid for my surgeries," she says, looking at Dare.

He nods. "Okay." He pushes his porkpie hat backwards on his head. "What else did Tayo say about me?"

"That you just had a breakup, and I should make you forget about her," she chuckles.

He chuckles as well.

"How'm I doing?" she asks.

"Not bad."

The waiter brings the shots and lays them on their table. Dare looks at the lime and salt on the tequila board. "What's the order again?" he asks her.

"Lick, shoot, suck."

"Okay," he replies, tipping some salt on the bridge between his thumb and index finger.

"We have to do it together," she instructs. She entwines her shot hand with his, they both lick salt before downing their shots and sucking on their lime wedges.

~

Dare and Mandy lie in his king size bed, kissing. His blinds are drawn down but the glare of the streetlights outside still creeps in. She rubs her hands on his torso, working them down to his boxers. She feels his hardness and sits on top of him, grabbing his penis through the parting in his boxers and inserting it into herself.

"No!" he exclaims, removing his penis. "Let me wear a condom."

"I don't do condoms."

"I don't know you."

The air conditioning goes off.

"Can you put the gen on? The smell of this your cheap lavender diffuser won't kill me," she says.

"I don't have a gen."

"What? What about an inverter?"

"No."

"Solar?"

He shakes his head.

"Are you fucking kidding me? What kind of grown man doesn't have an alternative power supply?" She hisses and starts to fan herself with her hands.

He gets up. "Let me get the rechargeable fan from the living room."

"Tell me you have something in the fridge to eat."

"I finished it."

"What? Couldn't you have ordered and kept?"

He fidgets.

"Don't bother about the fan, I'm leaving," she says, putting her clothes on.

He approaches her and puts a hand on her shoulder. "Stay, please. I'll make you happy, don't worry."

The electricity comes back on.

"Up NEPA," she says, giggling. They both laugh. She puts her bag down and removes her clothes again. "If they take light again, I'm going ooo."

"They won't take it. Think positive."

"You this man...if I knew your friend was winding me ehn, I wouldn't have agreed to meet you. What are you going to do for me?"

"I say don't worry. You're not leaving here empty-handed."

"You must make me cum too ooo. Can't just make me excited for nothing."

~

Tayo opens the door and sees Dare standing in front of him. Dare can see that Tayo is only wearing boxers.

"Bro," Tayo begins, looking behind Dare. "How did you enter the compound?"

Dare daps him, pulling him close for a hug. "Your neighbour was driving out, so I just closed the gate after him."

Tayo looks behind him into the flat.

"What's that mad smell? Did you hire a chef?" Dare asks, entering the open plan flat. Dare takes in the plain matte sofa, armchair, six-foot metal bookshelf and smart TV on a wooden console. "When did you get this?" he asks, pointing at the bookshelf. The kitchenette is in the right corner of the living room. He sees a woman with jumbo parted box braids stirring a wooden spoon in a medium-sized pot.

"Kemi? I almost didn't recognize you," he says. He looks behind him at Tayo before returning his gaze to her. "What are you doing here?"

Tayo grabs his arm from behind. "Dare, I was going to—"

"I'm not talking to you! I'm talking to her!" he replies, removing his arm from Tayo's grip.

Kemi switches off the gas cooker and looks at Tayo. She walks past the two of them and enters the master bedroom.

"You're not even going to talk to me?" Dare yells after her. He looks at Tayo and puts his hands on his head. "Is this why you pushed Mandy on me? To collect all my money? You didn't want my progress abi?

"Dare, it's been three months since Kemi lef—, I mean since you guys broke up."

"So how long has this been going on?"

"Let's go to the balcony, I don't want her to hear us."

"She might as well! I mean you're still going to tell her! Isn't she now your babe?"

Tayo sighs. "I was going to tell you this week. She called me a month ago to open a business account for her company."

"Which company? She works at the PR agency."

"She resigned. She registered a company immediately after."

Dare sinks to the sofa with his head in his hands. "Why her? You could have anyone."

"Kemi's a good woman. The truth is that I realized that all these other babes I was seeing were not it at all. Kemi cooks, she's domesticated, and she's content with who I am, while pushing me to be better."

"Fuck!" Dare exclaims, before getting up and leaving.

~

The barber trims Lati's goatee as Lati holds his hand mirror close to his face. "So much for the bro code," Lati says.

Dare laughs.

"Oh, so you're ready to joke about it now! I wasn't sure!" Lati laughs.

The three men are on the balcony of Lati's detached four-bedroom house on a cool July morning. Arched roofs dot the landscape of his estate. African warblers sing.

"This your app make sense die ooo—the barbing version of Uber!" Lati says.

"I was thinking of something that could make money daily," Dare begins, "I thought about food—I can't cook. I thought about a car wash—I worried about paying the guys who would wash for the first few months. And so, I started asking myself what other things do different men need to do every day? Shave or cut their hair! There are tens of thousands of barbing salons all over Lagos, so I asked myself, how can I stand out? I paid someone to design the app and started!"

Lati smiles. "What I love about it is how the barbers come to the customers."

"Uncle, that's the whole point. My selling point is that I wanted to make it convenient for men."

"Anyway, back to Kemi. The same way a woman might not have every single thing you want is the same way you don't have every single thing she wants. Love is a choice, not a feeling. It's loving the person even when they annoy you. Don't get me wrong, you still have to be physically attracted to the person. Other qualities are just as important. You were attracted to her, weren't you?"

"Of course."

"Ehen! She doesn't have to look like a porn star before she can be your wife. Trust me, in marriage you spend more time not having sex than having sex."

"So, you think I should beg her?"

"If you beg her, even me, I'll disown you."

Dare laughs. The barber laughs.

"She's gone. Now you know what to do going forward."

LOVE GROWS STRONGER IN DEATH

Where Swords and Missiles Fail

DAVID BEN EKE

Terrence was in a public taxi going for yet another interview with an NGO when he received a phone call. These interviews were part of his efforts at raising the 5 million naira he needed for his mother's radiotherapy—he had also posted her pictures to his scanty followers on Instagram, pleading for assistance. Posting those pictures felt so hypocritical because even he couldn't bear looking at them but somehow expected other people to do so—to take their time off scrolling through a feed of funny and interesting videos just to stare at the random picture of a mutated woman, and not only stare, but be moved enough to donate money.

On hearing Nurse Ada's first words over the phone, Terrence jumped out of the taxi, and soon, he was in a public bus, heading back to Primary Healthcare Centre, Mile 4.

The nurse's panicked voice kept replaying in his head: "Your mother is asking for you! She is asking for you!" He couldn't make sense of the frantic sentences that followed, and he is too disoriented to process what was happening. The only thought he could form was, "This can't be happening!"

Many times, he had imagined and prayed against this very moment, when he would be absent at the very moment he was most needed. He could almost see it now, his mother asking for him before she left, wanting to tell him one last story, direct him to the most powerful of Ekpeye herbs, instruct him on what to do with her wrappers, old and new. He could almost feel her chest heaving now, as her frail body struggled to breathe around the growth that covered her nostrils. *No, I can't. I can't bear to lose the one last person I have in this world.*

The bus he entered was full. He had hopped into it in motion with a finesse that growing up in Port Harcourt gifted him. How he was sitting now with a portion of the bus's seat enough for both of his tiny buttocks was a miracle, but one that didn't have his attention. Close to the window, he had a woman beside him (probably a market woman, going by the bag of pumpkin leaves she was holding). He was inhaling her strong stench. But even that—such a stench that could make one lightheaded—didn't have his attention. His mother was asking for him!

Normally, unpleasant ones, would trigger Terrence. But not this time. He seemed immune to the stench emanating from the woman beside him. While his body is in the bus, his soul had already reached his mother's wardroom at the hospital in Mile 4. His heart pounded in his chest, like a drumbeat of impending disaster. Goosebumps rose on his skin, whether from the cold breeze blowing through the broken window, or from the dark clouds gathering overhead whispering terrible prophecies about his mother's fate. He didn't want to listen to the words they spoke, but they lingered in his mind nonetheless.

He tried to distract himself. The bus was passing through Kala market, so he had many things to preoccupy his mind with: the dirty walls with cryptic graffiti drawings, which when deciphered could be premium lewd entertainment; Mobil filling-station with its long queue of cars; a little farther, a crowd gather around a teenage boy being beaten by a mob, a big black tyre hanging over his shoulders.

Terrence recognised one of the guys fighting on the right end of Mobil filling station. He was a former neighbour and a generator mechanic. Those days, the man had his house as both home and workshop, and Terrence and his friend Nonso used to joke that his children fed on generator spare parts and used small generators as furniture. This was funny because Terence and Nonso themselves had no furniture in their houses, used concrete floors as their beds, and spent most nights awake, battling the real owners of the bed space, insects. Their houses also looked the same then—big, brown planks assembled into amorphous structures, roofed with low-quality zinc sheets which blows off with the whirlwind during rainy seasons.

The Smelly Market woman beside Terrence sneezed, and her spittle landed on his hand. Now, she was beginning to clear the haze created by his worries with her extremely poor hygiene. He edged away from the woman and leaned on the bus's windowpane.

Had Nurse Ada thought to call Nonso's mother as well? She was closer to the hospital, her house being, like theirs, in Oroazi. He reached for his Nokia torch and tried calling Nonso's mother. She didn't answer. His heart resumed its drumming, rising to crescendos.

Nonso's mother was a superwoman. Even though her voice was strained when she called to inform him about his mother's diagnosis months ago, he was in awe of how much she had endured, how much she was still enduring, knowing by his own experience that the pain never quite went away. Two years ago, her husband was isolated and put on a ventilation machine, and when he was in dire need of oxygen, the hospital ran out of it. She was left to find cylinders of oxygen on her own. And she, of course, didn't find any. Because of that, her husband had died. Terrence wondered what his mother's hospital could be lacking now—syringes? Pain killers? Water? It was very possible in Nigeria that a hospital's lack of water could cost a person's life. Terrence shivered in his bus seat.

What Terrence found most heartbreaking about Nonso's mother's story was the fact that she was separated from her husband by disease before her final separation from life itself. She was a woman with the most beautiful gap-toothed smile, the finest cooking skills—oh, if she made Egusi soup for you eh!—and a heart of gold. But even she was not spared from the grief and loss brought on by the pandemic. A sorrow of parting with the hopefulness of reunion, then, a sudden quashing of all hope, a sudden wresting of a loved one from one's world.

The doctors had told Nonso's mother she couldn't see her husband or else she'd contract the virus he had. It was Nonso who told Terrence how she had retorted: "Contract wetin? So, I need to sign contract before I see my husband? Am I understanding myself right?"

Terrence briefly chuckled in the bus, hoping the market woman and other passengers behind him didn't think he was mad. Nonso had also described how his mother tugged at the doctor's collar and slapped a smallish nurse who refused to let her into the room where her husband was. Terrence remembered how much he and Nonso had laughed at the situation when the latter narrated the event. They had laughed in the dismissive manner typical of Nigerian men making it seem like nothing had happened to bring about Nonso's mother's reaction in the first place. It had become, to them— like many other sad realities in Nigeria—simple 'cruise' jokes, as though the man who had died wasn't the one who had saved them from their mothers' canes when they were younger; as though the man who had died hadn't sat them down and advised them to take JAMB and go to university when they were almost venturing into the fraudulent life of yahoo-yahoo.

Life's shege didn't stop with Nonso's father's initial isolation and eventual death. Terrence's brother, this guy who bathed in the rain with him, this guy who makes a cruise of every situation, this guy who often disobeyed his mother with him; this guy was next. Terrence dug into his dreads and scratched his scalp, removing his eyes from the road and fixating them on the seat in front of him. It was the driver's seat, and the driver was bald. He didn't snicker as he normally would at such a sight. He just stared. His mother's head had been shaved too during the chemotherapy. That was when baldness stopped being comedy. The bus had driven past Kala market.

It was last year that Terrence watched Nonso's devastating transformation. And, oh, it was no easy task. He visited him as often as he visited his own mother now—nothing less than 6 times a week—carrying food flasks of tasty Ogbono and Melechi-Ede that his mother used to make regularly. He always made sure to visit Nonso with the latest Nse Ikpe-Etim movies loaded on his third-hand iPhone 12 that he had bought from one of his OAU friends. Nse is Nonso's favourite actress. There were also Patience Ozokwo movies, as well as other movies that were trending at the time— Living in Bondage-remake, God Calling. That was before the iPhone 12 got stolen, and at a period when he had all the time in the world since the government had closed down all academic institutions because of Covid-19.

The alien that had invaded Nonso's body was a deadly form of pancreatic cancer. It was a cunning invader, difficult to detect and treat. Terrence got the devastating news about his friend in a late-night phone call, and immediately began searching for a way to help him. He scoured the internet and the depths of his own mind, but all he found was fear and despair.

'Communicate as usual,' one article online advised. 'Be ready to cope with mood swings,' another suggested. 'Don't ask *how can I help?*'

So, when Terrence returned to PH and was visiting Nonso's hospital, he had acted like he didn't cringe on the inside at Nonso's continual shrinking. He simply laughed when Nonso threw tantrums—very annoying tantrums—that'd on a usual day have had them wrestling each other like 5-year-olds.

'Push, push!' Terrence playfully urged Nonso when he suffered constipation.

'I dey born pikin?' Nonso managed to ask, jokingly, despite the pain he was feeling around his abdomen. And Terrence, wanting to be a good friend, had bottled in his laughter.

Nonso used to be so full of life and mirth, and oh, the laugh they could have had about the weird injection that went into his anus afterward, the fleet enema! Throughout Nonso's period of suffering, Terrence maintained a straight face, but now in the bus, he longed for an opportunity—even if it was just one more—to mock the hell out of his friend, insult his k-leg, sing songs about his fat, Pinocchio nose.

Nonso's face wasn't disfigured by the cancer. If Terrence had had the idea of starting a fundraiser for him then, his pictures wouldn't have been horrid enough to inspire people's pity and charity. His eyes only appeared yellowish, and so did his skin every now and then. Of course, this also left Terrence battling an urge to call him 'Yellow Ranger'. He never succumbed to the urge though; he just continued to yearn direly for that freedom again to be able to carelessly insult Nonso.

Terrence's bus halted at Wimpey junction. There was a traffic jam and Terrence peeped through the window but the traffic's end is invisible. He sighed and, whenever the traffic came to a stand-still for a long period, he partook in the grumblings of other passengers.

'Which kind traffic be this?'

'Hold-up every time for this Wimpey junction! Government no dey do their work at all!'

'God! Me, I don't have time oh! I am supposed to be somewhere by 3.'

This last remark came from one of those UNIPORT girls, giving-off bratty vibes even in a situation like this. Terrence turned back and eyed the girl's bony frame, then shook his head. She had an Ostrich-neck and scanty hair, resembling Vivian from his secondary school. Her cornrows didn't even extend past her orange, protuberant crown. The strips were pencilled lines and full stops on top and behind her oblong head. He'd have typed these to Nonso on WhatsApp if he were alive.

The bus remained in one spot. Terrence considered alighting, but there was no time to start walking from Wimpey junction to the hospital. Mucus would be rolling down from his mother's nose now, and she'd be screaming because of the pain around her face, and the pain of not having his hand holding hers. What if the black portion around her nose and under her right eye had ruptured? What if blood had started gushing out from it again as a side effect of her having chemotherapy that wasn't followed by radiotherapy? He needed to provide that money. He really needed to. But, how could he?

The money for the concluded chemotherapy had mainly come from a certain NGO, and the little contributions of his family's neighbours, his friends that cared, and whoever that was who put 50 naira in the Instagram fundraiser. He was grateful. The money needed now, 5 million naira (for the radiotherapy), was left to just him. That was the cost his mother's life had been reduced to.

He bit his nails, his eyes reddening. A man needs alcohol in this kind of moment, his father would have advised. When it feels like life is overwhelming and the whole world is crumbling or tumbling or collapsing, take two bottles or three, and see if you will stop until you're done with a crate of 12. There was no beer parlour to buy the drink now, neither was there time. And his mother would die the very second she smelt alcohol on his breath, for, to her, it would be a desecration to his body, the Almighty Lord's temple. Little did she know that he was now notorious across OAU for his ability to finish the most bottles of Heineken without staggering.

The bus moved forward in the traffic. He resolved to stay in. Besides, this was Port Harcourt—traffic here moved faster than it did in Lagos. He could wait in this one, unlike Lagos traffic that he constantly had to heal from whenever he attended parties with his friends, or went for a careers event.

He placed his head on the chair in front of him, and prayed as his mother would encourage; surely better advice than drowning in liquor and waking up to the unchangeable truth that reality was unchangeable. He wished, also, to break out in a round of tongues, but his tongue wasn't yielding. He said a prayer in his mind. First, he asked for mercy, then, that God should allow him to continue managing this one parent, then, that God should, in all His sovereignty, take his father into a deeper death and render his mother healthier. He pinched himself for praying such. A warm tear slid down his cheek, his head still bent over on the chair before him.

Terrence's father had said his goodbyes during the lockdown, only a year ago. It was the period Nonso was in the hospital. At least he was in closer proximity to his father when the man's own 'asking for you!' moment came. That day, Nonso had been scheduled for a chemo session, and as they planned it, Terrence's mother and Nonso's were the ones with him in the hospital. Terrence's father was home, and Terrence too, standing outside his family's house, talking with the gateman of the rich man whose house backed the shanty estate. That gateman smoked all smokables, but to Terrence's shock and disdain, hadn't come down with cancer.

The driver and conductor in Terrence's bus were screaming at another driver. They both came down from the bus and started charging towards the other driver—a very dark man with a bald head. Another bald head. Last year it was an object of comedy, but just nearly after about 365 days, it had come so close, and his view on it, the way he saw it, had turned a 180°. Sigh. Some passengers started coming down from the bus without paying, some went to calm the driver and his conductor down, and some stayed back in the bus, lamenting how the driver lacked *professionalism* and *sense of respect* for leaving his passengers to go and fight. No be only sense of respect.

Terrence placed his head on the chair again. On the day his father left, he rushed in upon hearing the man's voice: 'Yawe mini,'...cough, cough... 'Yawe mini.' His father was choking that day, and the pile of phlegm in his chest revealed itself in his crackly voice. Before Terrence could get him water to drink, he was on the floor, motionless, static, gone. Just like that.

His father's demise filled him with guilt because the reason he died was that he didn't get proper treatment, and his not getting proper treatment was as a result of the fear he passed on to both the man and his wife. Rumours said then, that if you went to the hospital with any sickness, you'd be admitted for Covid-19. It was alarming therefore to Terrence, that his father had catarrh, cough, and a blocked nose; he'd be isolated upon arrival at a hospital like Nonso's father had been isolated although his illness hadn't been explicitly named Covid-19.

Because Terrence so ably caught and spread this rumour, when his father's ailment worsened, their family's first resort was traditional means. His mother, an expert in that, travelled to Ahoada, and from the best of sources, plucked and brought home moringa leaves, orange leaves, and mango leaves. She cooked them in a big pot of water, and placed the boiling pot before Terrence's father who she and Terrence had sat on a small stool. They made him lean over the pot and covered him with a big bed sheet that they had borrowed from Papa James and John, their neighbour. Terrence's mother called this method, steaming.

'It can work! Ah! Those days me and my sisters go and sell akara for market, came back, and do steaming if we feel sick. It can work o.'

Terrence's father still died, and weeks after, Terrence was covering Nonso's face, too, with a sheet. When he confirmed his father's death that afternoon, he wasn't sure how to react. He envied everyone else as they trooped in and mourned, envied them for how well they expressed the hurt. He wanted to show he would miss his father too, if not in weeping and head shaking like his neighbours, in rolling and wailing like his mother, in quiet sobbing and arms folding like the rich man's smoker gateman.

Well, he also wanted to make his father proud—he wanted his father to be smiling in heaven (if that man made it there), nodding *that's my son being a man*. And being a man was not partaking in the emotional display; it was chesting the pain. Terrence tried, he chested, he chested, until he could no longer chest. And Nonso was in the hospital, too far away to share a mature man conversation that'd make room for the 'cruise' or the usual dry lamentations—the 'Only God knows' that incredibly, if feelings were fantasy, dissolved the questions; the 'Life goes on', and 'Na so life be' statements. He walked out of the crying scene, trekked to one of the incomplete buildings in Oroazi road, and poured it out. He cried till his ducts stopped shedding the tears, patting his chest till he was calm.

It was Terrence's powerlessness that ached him the most as he watched both his father and Nonso die. It was the same powerlessness that was aching him now—the 5 million naira he couldn't provide, the way he couldn't become tiny like Antman and counterattack the cancers around his mother's nose. He wished he could be half as nimble as his mother, half as capable of coming up with solutions for any trouble. Although her steaming hadn't worked for her husband's sickness, she had come through for him, her son, in too many instances, like when he cut his ear and she soothed his wound with python oil; when pimples sprouted on his face and she took Aloe Vera, mixed it with turmeric and her many other condiments, and won the war over his face; when a lump formed around his nipple, and with a native powder, she pressed it out of existence. Why was he so powerless against this cancer? Why couldn't he help?

When he and his mother spoke on the phone months ago before she was diagnosed with cancer, she believed she was having a mere catarrh.

'Om mbo uka-bushi. Bitter-cola and honey, I've drank three times since morning,' she had said, her tone reassuring. It was that tone he believed to be the highly-acclaimed 'motherly' tone—it always sounded like everything was under her control. He wondered if her tone was like that when she asked Nurse Ada for him. He had learnt now that the 'motherly' tone was false. It was simply there to comfort him. He only learnt this after his father was taken, and his mother stayed mute for months. That was when he saw she too was flesh and blood; she too was subject to life's exegesis. She too, his mother, Ina ye, could be played by life.

'Drunk o Ina me! Drunk!' he had corrected her over the phone that night, laughing. She had shrieked so loudly, and he, back in OAU, imagined her slapping Nonso's mother's lap, excited that this only son of hers was completing the education she didn't have the grace of getting. She normally took corrections well unlike his father who'd argue with him nonstop even when conspicuously wrong—like over the football game predictions on his betting slips, and whether or not Burna boy was from Ahoada. His parents were a special match made by God in heaven but marred by death on earth.

The driver and conductor finally got into the bus. It smelt like they had picked up even more repulsive odours from their banter. The whole bus was a zone of flavours, of smells oozing from the kings and queens of sweat and bad hygiene. It was getting to Terrence, but not as strongly as to pull him out of his ponderings. That's a lie. It had pulled him out, but he thought it immoral to succumb to its torture instead of the torture of his mother's asking for him and his not being there.

~

He contemplated what it'd mean if his mother died. He would be an orphan, alone in the world, unsupervised, not thought about. When he chased after women, following the itching of carnal flesh, he would no longer have the reassurance that his mother's prayers were going up to heaven on his behalf. He wouldn't have anyone to call when life became choking, when friends behaved nastily, when no one wanted to talk. He would have to revert to his constant dependence on staying in bed, drinking bottles of Heineken, stuffing his face in his pillow till he dampened it the way these cruel diseases had dampened his soul.

The barren woman of Ihuowo. He'd no longer hear about her. He'd no longer relish the sweetness of listening to that story of blessing and loss over and over again while staring at his mother's gentle grin and believing her exaggerated chronicles. He loved it every time his mother described the beautiful damsel made of palm oil. 'Ugbede, Nwo zo-zo, Ugbede Ehuda,' she'd call her.

This was a story he had constantly heard since he was a child, mostly on nights when his father slept early, when he would be seated with his mother—she on a chair, and he on their small stool—before the lit fire that the Agidi seller normally cooked with in the daytime. He would listen intently because every time she told the story, it was reborn with an unfalsifiable novelty, like God's pristine breathing upon man that remains pure as the cycle of birth and death go on for generations.

The barren woman of Ihuowo was an old woman who had no child. She'd go to her farm, forgetting her clothes outside, and whenever she returned after it had rained, someone would have removed them and arranged them in her hut. She observed this for a while until she went to consult with a soothsayer who told her it was a beautiful damsel made from her pot of palm oil, O'ga. He said that if she wanted to keep the girl in human form, she should pretend she had gone to her farm, lamenting her loneliness as she usually did, then hide and hold the palm oil girl from behind. If it threatened to rain, the soothsayer assured her, the girl would come out, and holding her from behind would keep her stuck in human form. The barren woman did this, and the girl remained in human form, living with her from then on, and helping her with her many chores.

The king saw the damsel one day and fell in love. He wanted to marry her. He told the barren woman of Ihuowo about his intentions, but she refused. The king insisted, and out of respect, the barren woman agreed, but told the king about the conditions associated with the girl: that she didn't go close to fires or come out when it was sunny. The king said he would respect these conditions, and took her in as one of his wives.

After some time, the king's other wives became jealous of the way he loved her. They plotted and agreed to cook a pot of soup, into which every wife must add an ingredient. As against the rule of not going close to fires, the palm oil girl was forced to add something to the pot of soup. She melted and spread through the compound of the palace, and then, everyone understood the reason why her conditions were in place.

A parrot was passing by. It saw what had happened and flew to inform the barren woman of Ihuowo about it. In anger of losing her dear treasure, she went to a native doctor that was known for spoiling things, Okoro-tashi— Terrence's mother always pointed out here that 'Okoro' was a word borrowed from the Igbos, whose meaning she didn't know, but 'tashi' was Ekpeye for 'spoil'. The barren woman brought Okoro-tashi to the King's palace, and destroyed everything in it—from his dogs and wives, to him, the king.

And the story like many other Ekpeye folktales ended with a song:

'Okoro-tashi-oo

Kiri-kiri yabiri-yabiri-ya kiri-kiri

Okoro-tashi-oo kiri-kiri-yabiri

Okoro-tashi ogbule-ogbo t'eze kiri-kiri yabiri-yabiri

Okoro-tashi ogbule ocho m'eze kiri-kiri yabiri-yabiri-ya'.

Terrence would never hear this story again. It was his mother's favourite. His heart ached. His eyes let out tears the way they used to when he was a child, flowing out rapidly, unrestrained. The smelly market woman was rubbing his back now, like a mother, quietly, tenderly.

For about one year, Terrence had missed the nights when he would sit and talk with his father about women and the soreness of marriage in his generation; he missed the nights they'd both plan betting slips and argue about whether Arsenal would beat Chelsea or Real Madrid and Barcelona's game would end 'goal-goal'. He missed the nights when he would sit with Nonso on the boot of his father's broken Volvo, staring at the moon and stars, sharing ideas on how to make money and daydreaming about wealth. Now that his mother too wanted to join the people that had waved goodbye, who would be his reason, his motivation for living?

His bus finally got to Mile 4 bus stop. He rushed out immediately, squeezing a 50 naira note into the conductor's hand in the process. He wanted to thank the smelly market woman for being motherly by rubbing his back, for showing him that, if, perchance, he lost this one last person in his life, there were many other persons in the world willing to show him love despite the sheges life was showing them too. He wanted to thank her for being mature as well, for not screaming in the bus that 'a whole man' was crying.

He ran into the hospital, Primary Healthcare Centre, Mile 4. He dashed past the reception, ignoring the 'stop skipping queue!' of some frustrated, ill individuals, and the 'gentleman please sign-in on the register' of the smallish receptionist. As he got closer to his mother's ward, he held on to a glimmer of hope that shone in the ordinariness of everything in the hospital—the pace of things that still moved the same, the smell of methylated spirit that still hung heavy in the air like every other day. He opened his mother's ward. It was then he saw Nurse Ada, the lady that had called him, a fair igbo woman he had once considered beautiful, once thought of approaching with a 'hey baby'. She appeared like a demon, an agent of the demonic realm, finalising for him a loss he would never retrieve. She was covering his mother's face with the hospital's blue sheet.

Tearless

AYO DEFORGE

1997

When the rains abated, everyone came out to play. The children taunted and tempted the waves. They stood by the edge of the ocean with their feet covered in white foam and waited until the waves rolled out close to meet them, before racing towards dry land. We wanted to play in the Atlantic Ocean but we were wary of its violent waves. They wielded immense strength, rose high above our heads and towered over us before crashing down with dreadful force.

Parents shouted the names of their children when they got too close to the shoreline. The women's voices were loud, the men's were sharp. Papa did not come to the beach with us. He never did anything with us. Mama sat on a wide mat under a palm tree. Sparkling white sand stuck to the soles of her feet. She was reading a romance novel, and at the same time, watching over the five of us. Each time she looked up from her book, she either shouted 'move back' or 'you are getting too close'. Tutu, who was in her arms, kept trying to grab her book or her reading glasses. Wale played football with some boys his height that he had met at the beach while Fola and some other children teased the restless waves. Lara and I sat side by side, our arms touching like Siamese twins. We were wearing the same pink swimsuit and our skin shone with the coconut oil Mama had rubbed on us. We sat silently with our feet buried deep in the wet sand so that we could feel its coolness against our skin. We sipped coconut water through a straw and watched the people around us.

A man with short dreads strolled by holding the reins of a dark brown horse. He stopped and tried to persuade us to ask our parents for a ride on his horse.

'We've already gotten a ride. You asked us when you went that way a while ago,' I said, pointing towards the direction he was coming from.

A moment later, a large wave rushed toward us and swept away our sandcastles. While I immediately began moulding new ones around my feet, Lara stared intensely ahead. I traced her gaze to where the sky and ocean merged into a symphony of blue, and after a while, I asked, 'What do you think is on the other side?'

She turned and looked at me but did not say anything. No longer expecting an answer, I scooped up a handful of sand and added it to my feet.

'America,' she finally replied, rolling her 'r', her voice gliding over the mesmerising melody of another huge wave as it crashed loudly against the shore.

'Move back Lami, Lara,' Mama shouted. 'You are too close.'

'But we haven't gotten up since we sat down here,' I argued.

Tired of rebuilding new sandcastles every time a brave wave reached us, I decided to hunt for pretty shells. I got up and wandered the upper beach, stepping on different footprints across the sand, fitting my feet into the big sizes, and erasing the smaller ones to print mine. Around me, several scared little crabs scurried in confusion, in different directions, looking for the nearest holes they could find. As I continued my pursuit of seashells, I pictured myself in my new school uniform walking with Lara. Mama had given me a leather watch because I had passed the Common Entrance exams in class five and would be skipping the next class to go straight to secondary school. I was happy because she'd also promised to replace my rubber sandals with Bata leather shoes.

After picking as many shells as I could hold with both hands, I knelt on the warm sand and filtered them, selecting those without blemishes and cracks.

I put them into a transparent plastic bag I had found on the beach and went to sit next to Mama on the mat.

'Would you like to carry Tutu?' she asked.

I knew that smile, the one she wore when she wanted me to do something I had the right to refuse. I stood and stretched out my hands toward my little sister. Eagerly, she came into my hands and grabbed my neck with her tiny arms. I laid back on the mat with my head propped up with towels, and then I sat her on my tummy.

'Fola, what did I tell you?' Mama shouted.

Startled, Tutu jumped and fell on my face. Afterwards, she giggled and tried to suck at my sticky skin. Digging my heels into the dry sand, I tried to lift her but my hands were not strong enough to hold her up for more than a few seconds at a time. Each time I lowered her, she would try to attack my eyes with kisses. It was at this point the doorbell rang thrusting me back into the present.

~

I closed the English textbook before me and rose from my chair to see who was at the door. The bell rang again just as I reached the entry. I opened the door to find Mama's brother standing there.

'Good morning, Uncle,' I said with a huge smile.

'Good morning, Lami,' he replied in a weak voice.

A faint smile crept to his lips and hung there. It refused to move up to his puffy eyes to lighten them up. For a few seconds, I stood and stared at him wondering why he was still dressed in his pyjamas and indoor slippers. I'd never seen him looking so dishevelled with an unkempt beard and uncombed hair. His light blue shirt which was unevenly buttoned exposed a part of his hairy chest and his dark blue dressing gown was all rumpled on his slender body. He looked as if he'd not slept for two days in a row.

Another strange thing I noticed was that he'd come without his distinct smell. Usually, when he came to visit, his perfume would fill the house and everyone could tell who had rung the bell before the door was opened.

'How are you?' he asked, averting his gaze. His voice too was different. It sounded like Mama's, after an eight-hour praise vigil at the Pentecostal church.

'I'm fine, Uncle,' I replied, unlocking the big black padlock on the burglar-proof bars that were fitted onto the door frame. I slid the bolt backwards as I opened the gate and let him in. He walked past me without giving me a bear hug as he would normally do.

'Today is Papa's birthday,' I whispered.

He nodded and said, 'Yes, I know.'

But he'd come with nothing—no cake, no gift, not even a birthday card. Nothing for us either. This too was unusual because he never visited without a packet of Choco Milo or Éclairs chocolate candies.

'How is Mama?'

'She is fine,' he replied quickly just as a strong breeze forced its way through the door of the front balcony, flinging it wide open. I shuddered as it brushed past me, momentarily leaving goosebumps on my body.

'Is everything all right?' I asked.

He nodded but still wouldn't look me in the eye. Instead, he pulled at the belt of his dressing gown which had been hanging loose and began to fasten it around his waist.

'Where is your Dad?' he asked without lifting his head.

'In his room,' I whispered again, 'He is ill. We wanted to come last Saturday like we promised Mama but he refused to bring us or let us take the bus.'

Without saying anything, he rubbed my short hair and walked into the living room. His strange attitude baffled me. I'd never seen Uncle Kay looking as serious as a detective at a murder scene. In times past, every time he was at the door and we asked who it was, to make us laugh, he would reply, 'It's Frank Spencer', impersonating the voice of the British actor from the television sitcom Some Mothers Do 'Ave 'Em. That afternoon, he wasn't in the mood to play the comedian. As I pushed the heavy padlock into place, I wondered if he was upset because Papa hadn't gone to visit Mama. I also wondered, if perhaps, Papa would allow us to return with Uncle Kay to Dolphin Estate to see Mama.

After shutting the door, I returned to the dining table where I'd been sitting. It was three years since the table was moved out of the dining room to take a temporary place in the corridor. Each time Papa and Mama had a fight and she stood up to him, to punish her, Papa would ban her from going into their room. Mama would then transform the dining room into a temporary abode until they settled their differences and she was allowed to move back into their bedroom. But their last fight lasted longer than all the others, and when they finally made up, Mama didn't want to go back anymore. She was finally tired of moving in and out, preferring to sleep in the dining room permanently.

Eager to tell Lara and Fola that Uncle Kay had come to visit, I packed up my textbooks and ran down the corridor. The last room on the right was the girls', and opposite, the boys'. I shared a room with my sisters, Lara and Tutu. It was painted in a glossy light blue like the rest of the flat. A brown wooden bunk bed was on the left. Pictures of Michael Jackson in different sizes—cut out from magazines and newspapers—were pasted on the wall of the lower bed. There was a brown cot by the wall opposite the door and a dark brown reading table on the right by the entrance. Just above the table was a corner shelf with two picture frames. One was of an unsmiling Lara and a smiling me standing right next to her. The other had been taken at our old apartment. It was a picture of my siblings and me sitting side by side on a sofa. Lara was the only one who was not smiling. Tutu was not in this picture as she'd not yet been born when it'd been taken.

'Uncle Kay is here,' I said as I burst into the girls' room.

Lara was sitting at the desk with a textbook open before her, however, she wasn't studying. Instead, she was playing a brick game on a handheld electronic device. As I'd hoped, my news pleased her. She turned to look at me and a small smile appeared on her lips. Although the smile swiftly passed, I was grateful for the opportunity to witness its brief passage. Without saying a word, she slipped her hand into the top drawer of the desk and brought out her writing pad and her new fountain pen. I could tell she was about to write Mama a long letter.

Lara loved to keep to herself. She spent her free time writing long letters which she kept locked away on her side of the wardrobe. No one knew where she hid the key. When she was upset with me, she would write me a letter. Same thing when she was upset with her classmate Chichi. She wrote Papa letters too but she never gave them to him. She also wrote long letters to her imaginary friends, amongst whom was Michael Jackson. Many times, she would not have lunch at school so that she could save up some money to buy stamps. On several occasions, I walked with her to Abiola Bookshop to buy envelopes and to the post office at Sabo to send letters to the Neverland Valley Ranch. Thereafter, she would check the letterbox each time she passed by it as if the mailman didn't come by only once a day. Did the letters ever get to California? Did Michael Jackson ever read them? Did the post office workers throw them out after reading them and laughing their heads off? I would never know as she never got a reply, nor did she give up writing to him. She was certain that someday he would reply and agree to adopt her and then she would change her name from Lara Davies to Pamela Jackson. I had dreams that he would want me too and that I would also change my name from Olamide Davies to Jennifer Jackson.

As Lara scribbled away on her writing pad, I felt proud of myself and gloried in my success at having brought her news that made her face break into its first smile of the day.

At school, several of the girls said that Lara and I could pass for twins although she is two years older. I didn't think we looked like each other that much. Although we have the same height, she was slimmer and much more beautiful. I'm light-skinned like Papa while she's as dark as roasted coffee beans, just like Mama. I was jealous of her soft and smooth skin which glowed when she rubbed on petroleum jelly after her morning bath. I wished that I had a dark complexion too so that no one could see the brown spots on the chicken skin behind my thighs, just like Papa. To me, Lara was a Yoruba goddess with long dark full hair. Her eyeballs were the colour of white pap and her teeth were whiter than the inside of a coconut. Lara's beauty was however always hidden behind a scowl. Often, she would drift into frightening moods and I would occupy myself with searching for what to say or do to see her take off her mask and reveal the artwork of Élédumaré. When I failed to get her spirits up, something which happened often, I would leave the room and let her be. Most times, I would pick a book and go to the dining table to read. At other times, I would go into the boys' room to chat with Fola. After Mama moved out of the master bedroom, she would let me come into her room to read or just sit and watch her sew. I didn't like to find myself drowning along with Lara in a river of despair.

As I was about to go to the boy's room to continue to spread the good news of Uncle Kay's visit, there was a tap on the door. Fola pushed the door slightly open and popped his head into the room. His eyes were reddish and he had lines printed on the right side of his face as if he had slept on rumpled clothes.

'Who rang the bell?' His voice was thick with sleep and his full eyebrows were raised curiously.

'Ooooh Betty,' I said, mimicking the British accent.

'Uncle Kay is here?' he asked, raising his brows even higher.

I nodded in response and a wide smile pushed up the corners of his lips, lightening up his eyes. He opened the door and stepped inside the room. Fola is two years younger than me and too tall for a ten-year-old. He had short curly hair and like Wale, his skin is the same tone as caramel cookies.

'Did he come alone?' Fola asked.

I was about to respond when a long loud cry came from the direction of the living room. It was Papa. His scream pierced through me as if a sharp object had been plunged into my chest. For several seconds, we remained transfixed until Lara dropped her pen and reading glasses on her writing pad and rushed to the living room. Fola unfroze and followed her. I ran after them.

~

Papa who had stayed in bed all morning was now sitting on a sofa. Before that day, I'd never heard nor seen him cry. I stood at the entrance of the living room afraid that when he would look up to find us watching him, he would get enraged and shout, 'gerrout!', then I would be the first to scurry down the corridor, as fast as my legs would permit me. But Papa didn't seem to care if we saw him in such an unmanly state. He held his head in his hands and his body shook as he wept.

'What happened to Mama?' Lara, who was standing in front of Papa, asked.

When Papa did not raise his head nor reply to her question, she turned to Uncle Kay, hoping to get a response to a question whose answer she already knew. Uncle Kay who was standing in front of the television also remained mute. His eyes were closed yet tears streamed down his face. Lara fell to her knees at his feet as if she was about to be anointed and ordained a minister. She covered her face with her hands and moaned, 'no no no no no', while shaking her head as if it would make the tragic news go away. My heart began to pulsate. After Papa screamed, it immediately dawned on me why Uncle Kay had red puffy eyes and why he'd come in pyjamas all the way from Dolphin Estate on Lagos Island.

Fola who was now sitting on the sofa next to Papa sobbed. He stared at the empty three-seater opposite him. Mama often lay there when she wasn't in her room. Some afternoons, when we returned from school, she would be lying on the blue leopard-patterned three-seater sofa because the living room had better ventilation. I remember her frail body in an oversized Bubu gown, her dried thin lips, her eyeballs that had taken refuge inside their sockets, and her scalp that looked as if it had never been graced with long relaxed hair. I also remember the first time she died on that sofa. Lara had shaken her back to life while screaming 'Mama, wake up! I beg of you! Please, wake up!' I remember the look on Mama's pale face when she was resurrected. I can still hear her saying, 'I was almost gone but I fought hard because I don't want to leave my children. If I die, your father won't take care of you'. Lara and I had held her hands and tried to comfort her, and at the same time, we'd struggled to hold back our tears. As Mama's breathing became easier, I heard her muttering, 'If I die, my children will suffer'. She kept repeating this in a low voice until she fell asleep.

Uncle Kay didn't need to tell us what had happened to Mama. We didn't need to hear it spelt out either. We knew that she'd been battling for her life and that death had won.

Mama had been ill for about two years. Grandma moved in with us in February to take care of her. Mama had stopped having house-help. She never told me why but Lara told me it was because Papa always sleeps with them. Two months after Grandma arrived, she returned to Dolphin Estate taking Mama with her. She needed assistance to take care of her daughter and Papa wasn't giving her a helping hand. Mama also needed a change of environment. Papa must have been glad about the decision because he came home early every night after they moved out. He'd also been glad when Grandma first arrived because he no longer had to give Mama her bath or disinfect the big lumps that had grown on her left thigh.

The last time we'd seen Mama had been two weeks before. Papa didn't drop us off in front of the block of flats where Mama was living with her parents. Instead, he stopped us on Osborne Road's expressway bridge which passed by Dolphin Estate. He and his elder sister, Mama Ola, were going to see the piece of land he owned in Agbara Estate. Papa had said that he wanted to start building his own house because he paid too much rent where we lived. Mama Ola sat in the passenger seat; Tutu who was sitting on her lap was fast asleep. Mama Ola talked non-stop. She pulled down the visor so that she could do her makeup. She rubbed some talc powder on her dark face and then applied her green lipstick over and over again until it turned red on her lips. From time to time, she would scratch her palms and interrupt her own monologue to say, 'Oh money is coming. Somebody is bringing me money.'

When we arrived at Mc Gregory Canal, Lara, Fola and I jumped from the bridge and landed on a heap of refuse that the residents had dumped on Corporation Drive. Afterwards, Mama Ola passed Tutu down to me. After we watched Papa drive off, we didn't go straight to see Mama. Instead, we went to Isolo Street to visit an old baboon locked up in a cage. We'd not eaten our bananas at breakfast but hidden them in our backpacks because we wanted to give them to the baboon that had no hair on its buttocks. After feeding the poor animal, we said our goodbyes to it many times before heading for our destination. While Lara walked ahead of us, Fola and I held Tutu's hands and pulled her up every four steps so that her feet didn't touch the ground. Excited, she laughed loudly and kept repeating, 'again, again'.

Tutu refused to go into Mama's room all through our visit. She would stand by the door and peep in, then she would give Mama a shy smile and call her, 'Baba'. Each time Mama invited her to come in, she would run away only to come back a while later to repeat the process. This made Mama cry. She looked skeletal and all her hair had fallen out during chemotherapy. Tutu didn't recognise her anymore. When Aunty Jire, Mama's only sister, returned from choir rehearsal, she stood at the window so that she could alert us when Papa drove up the street. We watched movie after movie, ate non-stop and had catnaps. The sun had already set when Papa returned to pick us up. He and Mama Ola still wouldn't come up to see Mama. Papa was angry with Mama and her parents for not allowing him to see her the last time he'd visited. He said that he'd been told that she was asleep but he'd heard her coughing for a couple of minutes.

'She can't fall asleep when she coughs like that,' he'd said. 'She didn't want to see me. They didn't want me to see her and I'll never set foot in that place again!'

When Papa honked the first time, Tutu was sleeping on the three-seater sofa in the living room. Fola, Uncle Kay and I were playing Scrabble at the dining table while Lara was listening to Michael Jackson's songs in Uncle Kay's room. We all rushed to Mama's room to say goodbye. When Papa honked a second time, I was kissing Mama's wet face. The strong smell of antiseptic solution and Robb ointment filled my lungs. I placed another light kiss on her thin hand. It was nothing like the hand I used to know. Her nails were clubbed and her skin was as thin as cellophane film. 'Don't cry Mama,' I said, resisting the urge to cry too. 'Saturday will soon be here again.'

For several hours that day, she'd sat up in bed with her back against the wall, braced by pillows. When she told us she would be returning home anytime soon, her eyes were no longer those that had been dimmed by cancer. They were like those of a survivor—they beamed with hope. When she'd said that God had healed her, I believed her. Not because the lumps that had sprung up in every part of her body had now disappeared but because of the dream she'd had. In the dream, an angel dressed up like an Indian had sat beside her on the bed and had pulled out a pin from each lump. After she woke up from the dream, her body no longer burned with pain. She'd said that she felt better and stronger every day since then. I didn't doubt her for a second. I believed she was returning home soon and that everything would be back to normal. 'I can't wait for you to be back home so we can dance to Days of Elijah, I'd said to her. She smiled and curled her hand around mine, threading her fingers in between mine and tightening them for a few seconds.

When Papa honked the third time, my siblings and I ran out of the apartment and down the stairs. We looked forward to the following Saturday when we would return to Dolphin Estate to see Mama and everyone else. But when Saturday finally arrived, Papa refused to take us to see Mama. He also refused to allow us to go by bus. Yet, we'd been good all week so that he wouldn't have any reason to punish us by preventing us from going the coming Saturday. So as Papa cried that morning, hiding his face in his hands, I couldn't tell if the tears came from his soul.

'Did it happen today?' I asked Uncle Kay.

My voice didn't let me down. It remained the same. It didn't tremble. It hadn't thinned with anguish nor had it been burdened with unshed tears. Uncle Kay nodded in response.

Tutu, who had been sleeping in Papa's room, walked into the living room, holding a pink stuffed bunny rabbit. She stood still in the doorway, holding her favourite pink blanket in one hand and looking frightened as she watched the faces of everyone in silence. When she walked up to Papa and touched his knee, he uncovered his face, looked at her and burst into fresh tears. She joined him with robust tears running down her face, even though she didn't know why he was crying. Uncle Kay picked her up and cuddled her. I squeezed my eyes shut. I wanted to break down and cry too. I wanted to weep like everyone else around me. I wanted to have tears running down my cheeks but I couldn't. Deep down, I felt as though if I let myself be overwhelmed, I would be signing a binding contract with God that Mama could die. I would be releasing her to death and testifying that I could manage without her. To me, grieving her meant that I would be giving up on her and agreeing to let her go. Mourning became an irreversible mistake and my inability to cry, a blessing.

I was going to be twelve in nine days and I wanted Mama to wake me up to the smell of baking cake as she always did on our birthdays. To wake us up, she would either sprinkle cold water on us or tickle under our feet. Then she would begin to sing 'Happy Birthday to you' in her beautiful voice.

A pain stabbed my chest as these memories flooded back. Then it grew worse when a storm of guilt seized me. I was suddenly convinced that God hadn't heard my prayers because I hadn't prayed hard enough. Many times, I had dozed off during prayers for Mama's healing and when I awoke at the end of the prayers, I would ask God to forgive me for my lack of concentration. I felt anger stir within me, against me. I should have prayed all night and every night until she got healed. Next, I felt my anger steer towards Mama. She too should have kept her part of the promise of not abandoning us. She should have fought harder to stay alive.

Suddenly, the world began to spin fast around me or maybe it was me who was swirling around in my head. I managed to walk to the three-seater sofa where Uncle Kay was sitting and cuddling Tutu who had stopped crying and gone back to sleep. I settled down next to Uncle Kay and looked around the room. Papa too had stopped crying but he still wouldn't keep his head up. Fola sat still and his eyes were fixed on the white ceiling. Lara was the only one who was still crying. Her cries were soft and weak as she lay on her side, curled up like a cat.

I knew instinctively that I had to get out of there. I'd done it several times before to escape pain, and most of the time, it worked. I pulled my legs up, rested my chin on my knees and put my arms around them. Then I detached myself and broke away. I became a little cloud up in a dark sky, watching them from above, soaring higher and higher.

Blue

MOHAMMED BABAJIDE MOHAMMED

The night death came for mother was a cold, dark, and rainy one. It started like any other night. Mother made me my favourite meal for dinner, put the cat out, and retired to her room. At first, I thought it was my drowsiness, but I could have sworn I saw a shadow latch on to her as she left my room. A black, faceless void that oozed of gloom and despair.

Of course, at the time, I did not yet know what fate had in store for her, but nevertheless I felt a sense of dread as her frail hand closed the door that day. As I lay in the darkness with silence, I began to allow my mind to drift everywhere and nowhere in particular. My thoughts had not roamed too far when I heard a loud thump from the other room. Death had arrived at our home.

With what was left of my strength, I lifted myself from my bed. Despite my thunderous headache and foggy mind, I embarked on the herculean task of thinking. Slowly I made my way out of my room, dragged myself down the corridor and into mother's room. I placed my hand on the doorknob and a silent prayer flapped its wings off my lips. She was all I had left, so I prayed she was safe. Amidst this prayer, a lack of conviction lurked in my belly.

I pushed the door, overwhelmed with dread, but strengthened by purpose.

Mother had slumped on the floor, her face visible from the low lighting on the dark skies. I felt a cold wind rush past the room. Death had just ushered her soul away...

I willed myself to move closer to her. I edged ever closer to the frail body on the floor. Her body was as lifeless as the clothes she had on. I knelt beside her and wept.

As lighting struck, I saw my mother's face clearly for the first time. Her eyes were fixed on the ceiling. Her lips slightly parted.

This grim moment would stay with me forever.

I recalled my first memory. It was mother's face. She had been with me from inception. She ushered my warm frail hand to life, and now I held on to her cold frail one in death.

Later when the ambulance arrived, Mother was officially pronounced dead at the hospital.

That was two years ago.

~

I still remember that night as though it happened moments ago. I am unable to shed the grief. It has lingered with me for long. Now it is only through the veils of grief and sorrow that I am able to recall my love for my mother. Often, I sit alone on the lawn, admiring the skies, searching for her...

Apologies... Or perhaps, might the phrase 'pardon me' be more appropriate? For you see, I *must* insist on an apology for the space I have left at the start of my tale.

You may well call these bare lines moments 'seconds of hesitation', where I delay a commencement, for I have trouble finding a perfect beginning.

Should I have started with the winds? The gentle breeze that sings beautifully, like an orchestra tailored specifically for my whims. Or should I have scribed a beginning from the swaying trees? Their movements above description by tongue of any illustrator? Their beauty far beyond the reach of pencil or paintbrush of even the most gifted artist? Or might I have even started with the woman that sits beside me? Her visage veiled by golden gleams. Her emaciated face deprived of smile. Her wrought fingers playing the degraded strings of her tarnished guitar?

My life starts with six stings. A beautiful piece of symphony bred from the core of my mother's guitar. My life starts with her, the lost maiden that sits beside me, her presence unfelt, her sight unseen, but here she sits, like a blemished memory.

As a kid, I grew up with my mother. My father's face is unknown to me, he left before I was born. Mother used to tell me stories about him, but I got the gist: a heartless drunk who was more devoted to his bottle than his own family.

Mother was a writer, but her books did not sell much, so she found solace in the strings of the guitar, dwelling in a world of her own.

I on the other hand lived a normal life—or as close to normal as I could be. Due to my 'slight' intelligence, I was the very best in all aspects in life, and I had a promising future, contrary to the destiny fate had planned for me.

At first mother did not take my complaints of headaches and drowsiness seriously, but a particular burst of intense agony on one fateful day made her see reason. She took me to the hospital (very much against my wishes for I detested the hospital in all aspects), and there, the doctors diagnosed me with 'a tumor in the cerebral cortex'. They further went ahead to shatter my dear mother's heart by stating that it was inoperable, and that I had less than a year to live.

Mother did all she could to abate my suffering and ease my grief. Everything a loving mother could do for her dying child. Her efforts did very little to ignite my spirit.

Each day seems to bring new pain. Each night ushered in new misery. I know a day will come when I have no days left, gone never to see the sun, never to feel the winds, confined to the dark wooden world of my own coffin.

Mother had died of a stroke. Perhaps she had thought death would bring her peace, leaving her doomed son to spend the rest of his days without a parents' comfort, friendless and alone, cursed to wander without hope. For a long time, I was angry at her for leaving me at my time of greatest need, but as the weeks passed, my exasperation was elated...for I know now that she has finally found peace. So, with great effort, I relinquished her from my dreams and accepted that she's indeed free.

And now, sitting on this green field and watching the skies, I muse to the rhythm of the guileful winds. Mother sits beside me, free from the shackles of life, yet a prisoner of my memories. She plays her guitar, drawing my body away from my pain, and my mind away from my sorrows, until I am drowned in love.

She looks at me. Her thin face stretching tight across her skull as she brings forth a smile.

I stare at her for an eternity. She seems to stare back beyond a shroud of grief. And then she begins to fade, until she's but a blur, and then she is gone.

Auld Lang Syne

ELISHA OLUYEMI

NOW — 15 DECEMBER 2023

Sometimes, our end is an orgasm, the joy of God when he crafted Adam, the pride of Adam when he entered Eve. The euphoria in Doctor Faustus when the devil held his hand. Helen of Troy analogizes it well, this dark phenomenon—because, the moment she stopped walking alone, I mean the moment butterflies began to flutter in her belly, she choked, like a wild lover asphyxiated at the peak of an intercourse.

"Aren't we all little tragic things?" I whisper into the wind while holding the hand of my lover as we walk down the pavement that leads us to nowhere—nowhere because sometimes, we have to lose ourselves.

I don't hear a response from my lover, and I don't bother to repeat the question or glance at her face to confirm a reception. We are all humans after all—full of diversities. That name, human, binds us together, whether we are dead or alive. Humans, chess pieces. Victims of a recurring fate. My lover is a trunk, and the wind passes through her body as we walk ourselves on.

"Dipo," she calls me with a drawl.

I stop and gaze into her eyes. They are bright and sheeny, as innocent as a child's. The smile on her lips spreads to her ears, and she seizes my arm and locks her arm in. Then her head rests on my shoulder. My eyes settle on her head. I kiss her hair, I inhale the smell of peppermint, I moan. And silently, I curse the moment of loss—the phenomenon that makes a man's phallus limp.

My lover tilts her head and looks up, into my eyes. Then she unlocks our arms. "Shouldn't you stop now?"

She smiles.

She gazes into the distance beyond the lamp-lit street, beyond the endless stretch of this pavement. She smiles again, shakes her head, parts her mouth in a giggle—again like a carefree child—and she turns away.

She begins to run. My lover.

"Sola!— Sola, don't!"

24 MAY 2021

We sit at a round table that is covered in red. An ottoman rests beside me, and on it is a basket bearing a bouquet of flowers and a gift box.

Sola keeps her eyes on me as she sips from the coffee cup.

"Something's different about you today," she says, setting the cup on the saucer. She tilts her head, smiling. "I can't quite place it."

"Isn't it natural?" I shrug. "The day's different after all."

She looks around. And I follow. Of course, the restaurant is quiet; servers and guests, everyone is minding their business. There's no artist to entertain, except for the soft Janis Joplin's *Me and Bobby McGee* playing in the background.

Sola shrugs. "I don't see what's different." She leans forward and winks. "Care to tell me?"

I also lean forward, smiling. "You really like to play, don't you?"

"Of course I do. But," she shakes her head, "this time, I really have no idea."

"Oh really?" I sit back. I've been hearing of things like this; but here it is, happening to me. I laugh. It's the perfect circumstance after all. Don't we all scream because we don't 'see it coming'? I rise from my seat, throw my hands up, and clap, whistling, halting the tranquil in this hall.

Then, I step away from the table.

The managers understand the cue. Immediately, Janis Joplin's music peters out and is replaced by Simi ft. Adekunle Gold's *Happy Birthday*. I see the heavily-bearded disc jockey nodding with a grin. The hostesses are approaching us with a chocolate cake and balloons and smiles. My lover is a child at heart, and she deserves this much. The other guests begin to groove to the music, some waving their hands, some singing out the lyrics.

I turn my attention to Sola hoping she can now see that the atmosphere is different, that the entire hall is rocking because of her. All these smiling faces, all these bright hearts. *Just for you.*

But Sola's gaze wanders away, her shoulders sagging. And when she looks up at me, there's a bulge in her eyes, a glimmer of amusement. She's like a random guest witnessing someone else's birthday-surprise event and musing, *Aw, what a lucky woman!* She looks at me and shakes her head, mouthing something I do not hear. I hurry to her side and lean over. Before I can say a word, Sola blurts out, "It's not my birthday, Dipo. And it's not yours, is it? You celebrated last month."

I freeze, my eyes locking with hers. "Shouldn't you stop the joke now?"

I glance at the hostesses grooving while bearing the cake and balloons. Someone already set a wine bottle on the table; people are taking pictures. "Sola. Today is your birthday. You didn't forget, did you?"

I try to laugh.

She giggles. "The situation is awkward already, Dipo, but, well I can just play along."

We both stand upright. Sola begins to beam, her eyes dilating. One hand levitates to her chest, the other to her mouth. Then she hugs me tight. She waves to the hostesses, spreads her arms and embraces them. Calls of 'Happy Birthday' course from the guests, and Sola waves back at the well-wishers.

"Happy birthday to you," I sing for her. Light the candles on her cake and watch her blow the flames out.

~

"Played it well for you, right?" Sola laughs as she reclines in the passenger seat and puts on the seatbelt. "I mean, what were you thinking?"

I gaze at her, resisting the urge to step out and slam the car door. "It's not funny, Sola. You're making me feel bad."

"Ah... I'm sorry."

"Tell me, what is today?"

She looks away. "My fake birthday."

"May 23rd, Sola. We celebrated your birthday on this date last year. All through high school, all through our undergraduate years, May 23rd has always been for you. So what has changed? Why did we come to this restaurant in the first place?"

Her face turns in my direction, a frown forming on it, but she is not looking at me.

"Sola? And I didn't celebrate a birthday last month. My birthday is in December. We both know this. I don't understand what joke you were trying to make inside there. I almost felt embarrassed. A guy who arranges a surprise party for his fiancee on the wrong date, huh?"

"My birthday is not today! What is wrong with you? And what is all that talk about birthdays in high school and university? When did I meet you?

Last month, Dipo. Last month!" She tugs her hair behind her wavy hair and looks out the tinted window. "Let's go. We should even rest first before talking about this, cause I don't understand."

For a moment, I feel like a madman. Like an idiot. But I refuse to act like one. I only turn the ignition and press the brake pedal. And as we drive to my apartment—Sola has recently moved in with me—I remain quiet and keep my gaze ahead. Until the moment when I begin to sense a shock:

"Are you okay?" Sola asks me in the most innocent voice, her eyes scanning my face. She reaches for my face, caressing my chin. "Talk to me, dear."

24 MAY 2021

6:10 AM

I launch Google Photos and browse the grid of albums I recently created on the software:

> —*Family*
>
> —*Childhood*
>
> —*2018 Birthday*
>
> —*2019 Birthday*
>
> —*2020 Birthday*
>
> —*High School*
>
> —*University of Nigeria*
>
> —*Me & Sola Moments*
>
> —*Sola's Birthdays*
>
> —*NYSC*
>
> —*Randoms*

Sola has been a part of me as far as I can remember. And so she has a place in all the albums in my library. I open the Family folder, and there she is, standing with my mom and dad and two sisters as we pose for a family photo on New Year's Day. She was barely ten at that time. I was eleven. My mum, beaming a smile, had her hands on Sola's shoulder in an affectionate way. Sola was grinning in that picture, one of her incisors missing. She wore beaded long hair and was twirling the end of her side locks. She lived close by with her family who were our friends—sadly, her parents are now deceased; they both died in an accident on one of the days she was spending time in our house. That day, as Rod Stewart's *Auld Lang Syne* played, Sola held my Mum's hand, whining, "Allow me to join the photograph. I will marry Dipo." Everyone laughed, but my eyes were on Sola, my mind supplicating the Deity, that this carefree little girl be truly tied to my future. I walked to Dad's side and raised his arm, letting it rest on my shoulder, and I took a deep breath and mumbled, *Amen.*

My birthday is not today! What is wrong with you? And what is all that talk about birthdays in high school and university? When did I meet you? Last month, Dipo. Last month!

I throw back my head, put my phone away. "Gosh." I pick it back up and browse the folder named *Sola's Birthdays.* The timeline features photos dating eight years back. Many of the old photos originally were physical copies scanned and archived on my cloud storage. And in almost all of them, I am there by Sola's side. Not only that... Her birth photos are time-stamped *May 23.*

My birthday is not today! What is wrong with you? Sola's voice echoes in my head.

8:40 AM

Sola comes to me, waving her phone in my face. She's all smiles, although her face looks puffed up thanks to a long night of sleep. She'd fallen fast asleep as soon as we came back home last night. "The birthday surprise yesterday was one of the best, you know," she says, grinning. She sits on the arm of the one-seater chair I'm sitting on and snakes a slender arm round my neck, kissing my cheek.

I gaze at her up close. My jaws clench on their own accord. *Sola, what's going on with you?*

"I was going to upload a WhatsApp status today, and I saw all the pictures. You know, it was as if I was drunk all through yesterday and needed to see something to trigger my memories, hehe."

She shows me a picture in which I'm presenting her a bouquet and a gift box. "I like this one in particular. Awn, you're so sweet." She kisses me again. "There are videos, too. See eh, our wedding is in fourteen months, right—"

"Sola?" I call quietly, my mind chaotic. *Yes, our wedding is fourteen months, but...*

"Why? You look distressed. Are you okay?"

1 JANUARY 2022

New Year's Day.

Sola wakes up grabbing a blanket and wrapping it around her. She wakes up casting furtive glances around. She was fast asleep in my arms all night. She was calmly in my mind as I pictured the new year, how it will be spiced with a heavy dose of Sola.

But the colour of her face at the moment is white. Colours appear boldly on white. Sola's face is a graffiti of alien emotions. She is bawling, she is screaming, she is throwing things, breaking things, and repeating: "Who are you? Where am I? I'll report you! Who are you!"

When the spiked heel of a stiletto grazes my head and draws blood, I hurry towards Sola and embrace her so tight she must be feeling tied up. I struggle to keep her in this shape for several minutes, telling her nonstop, "I'm Dipo, your lover. Remember me, Sola. I'm Dipo, your lover."

Soon, she turns limp, her body warm. My nostrils ache with the sensation of grief.

~

Sola wakes up. It is evening.

"I feel tired, Dipo," she tells me when she opens her eyes to see me seated by her on the bed.

I sigh and clasp my hands in relief. "Sola mí."

15 DECEMBER 2022

It's my birthday today. I'm 32. Sola isn't here with me, at least for now. We ought to be married by now. But Sola wants to have a good job before tying the knot.

Today, she has a job interview that will take the whole day if she impresses early enough.

"It's the biggest law firm in Abuja, so I'll need to do a lot to prove I'm worthy," she told me yesterday.

She informed me again this morning: "If I get this job, Dipo, I swear, I'll come home screaming," she said, buttoning up her white shirt, "I'll scream so loud our neighbours will hurry out. They'll want to see what has happened to Dipo's bae."

She turned to me and grabbed my pyjama top by the collar, making a face. "And I'll tell them, see what the Lord has done!"

I bursted out laughing at this and poked her nose lightly. "You don't have the balls."

"If a lawyer can't be *bally* and dramatic, then she is a bad egg to the bar," she laughed.

"*Ball-ly*, yeah," I giggled. "But I—"

"You will see."

"We'll celebrate my birthday later in the night, then?"

"Yeah, after I come home screaming. But em, Dipo, don't call me until I'm back, you get? In fact, I'll have to use Flight mode. But you understand the reason, right?"

I nod, pulling her close. "Don't worry, I'll let you stay focused. I'll wait for you."

It's night now. And I'm still waiting to hear Sola's screams. If it happens, then I'm certain that even I won't be able to contain her joy; my birthday celebration will be heavily spiced with the celebration of someone's dream job. It will be perfect—two lovers living a fulfilled life.

My phone rings.

"This is Inspector Lati, calling from Maitama Police Station, Abuja. Are we on to Mr Dipo Laniyan?"

~

Sola is sitting on a bench in the lobby of Maitama Police Station. She hasn't committed a crime.

An officer had told me: "We found her standing aimlessly in the middle of Shehu Shagari Road. Not only was she obstructing traffic, she was also endangering her own life. What if something had happened to her?"

I hurry to Sola and crouch before her, cupping her hands. "Sola?"

"She has been here since afternoon, sir," the officer's voice interrupted me. "She didn't seem to know where she was coming from or her destination. She couldn't tell us anything until this evening when we decided to check her bag for any means of identification. We found your number in her emergency contacts. We couldn't reach the others."

I ease up my feet with clenched fist. "Really? You guys ehn?" I can hear the tremble in my voice. "Why didn't you check her bag since morning? Why did you have to wait until now? Do you think she's nothing just because—"

"Di-po," Sola calls quietly.

I crouch before her and touch her face. "Sola? Are you okay? Why didn't you call me? Did you lose your way?"

"I don't think she lost her way—"

"Can you leave us!" I snap at the nagging officer and redirect my attention to Sola. With a tender touch, I run my index finger along the contours of her face, tucking away strands of stray hair. "Sola, we should go home."

~

Sola says nothing even after my car pulls up outside the apartment. She says nothing even after we enter the living room. After a long time looking spaced out and unresponsive to my tender words and gestures, she finally stands up and walks into the bedroom.

After a while, I go to check on her. She is sleeping.

I walk to my reading table, power on my MacBook and check the storage for a copy of the cover letter I'd helped Sola write. I find the contact information of the law firm's office. And I call.

It doesn't connect. Of course, it won't. Office hours are over.

I call the officer from Maitama Police Station.

"I was trying to explain things properly but you were impatient," Inspector Lati says.

"What else did you find?" I ask him.

"We have standby medical professionals for trauma cases, Mr Dipo. They examined her when she began exhibiting symptoms of behavioural impairment. And although she's not physically affected by anything, our professionals believe she should get some therapy. If you wish to see the report—"

I end the call-in worry. *Is Sola depressed?*

My stomach churns. *Suicidal? Did she really go to the highway to...?* It doesn't make sense. And even if it does, I should rule it out.

I sit by Sola all night, my eyes on her face. The more I gaze at her, the more the memories of her overwhelm my fears. So, I decide to remain by her, at least until she wakes up. No new-job celebration. And no birthday revelry, for the first time in my life.

15 DECEMBER 2023

It's my birthday today. I'm 33. And, I tell you, it's been one year since Sola last spoke. She eats, she moves around, she watches TV, she orders magazines. But she barely steps out. She writes a lot too, and she locks her writing away in a mini safe that used to belong to her father. I don't know what she writes, and I might never know.

The day after the incident, I called that law firm again. It was during office hours this time, so it connected. The desk officer checked their records. They said Sola didn't appear for the interview. "She was one of the first five people scheduled for the morning examination," the young man explained, his voice heavily nasal. "Our director had even sworn to back her personally. Miss Sola Adeyeye had a huge chance—"

I hung up. I didn't need the remaining information. I just wanted to know if anything could connect Sola's strange appearance on the highway and the job-hunting at her dream law firm. Perhaps, she had performed badly during the interview and had lost control of her disappointment. However, it turned out there was none.

So where did the change come from? Why did it come to my lover?

There is a creaking sound behind me.

"Don't move," came the voice.

I hear the rumble of a boom bass speaker. I hear the robotic call, *CONNECTED.*

Then I hear the soft piano chords kicking off Rod Stewart's legendary soul music, Auld Lang Syne, a song often played on New Year's Eve in many parts of the world to mark the end of the year and to usher in the new. I shake my head. *Auld Lang Syne. Times Long past.*

Should old acquaintance be forgot?

And never brought to mind?

Should old acquaintance be forgot

And the days of Auld Lang Syne?

"Happy Birthday," the voice comes, this time, clearer.

I turn sharply without needing instruction.

"Sola," I cry. She stands before me, smiling, wearing beaded hair with locks dangling by both sides of her face. She had been inside all evening making her hair, I see. This reminds me of her childhood. Of the times when life wasn't strange.

I spread out my arms and hug Sola tightly, sniffing sobs and remaining like that for a long time.

"Let's take a walk... Dipo," she says to me, smiling calmly in my face.

~

"Aren't we all little tragic things?" I whisper into the wind while holding the hand of my lover as we walk down the pavement that leads us to nowhere—nowhere because sometimes, we have to lose ourselves.

I don't hear a response from my lover, and I don't bother to repeat the question or glance at her face to confirm a reception. We are all humans after all—full of diversities? That name, human, binds us together, whether we are dead or alive, whether we are lost or in the right place. Humans, chess pieces. Victims of a recurring fate. My lover is a trunk, and the wind passes through her body as we walk ourselves on.

My lover tilts her head and looks up, into my eyes. Then she unlocks our arms. "Shouldn't you stop now?" She smiles. "You have tried."

Soon, I see her back melting into the darkness ahead. And as I call her name, running after her, we slip further into it.

The Typewriter

AISHAT ADESANYA

I love this garden for many reasons. Its beauty and bright colours make it seem as though it is straight out of a fairy tale. Its seclusion, nestled in our favourite part of Abuja.

Qub and I like to come here to take in the exotic flowers around the open space. The setting sun gives the waters sitting beside the garden a mysterious but satisfying look. I enjoy spending alone time with my Qub in such beautiful solitude.

'Mon Cherie,' he calls me as we sit underneath a tree in the middle of the garden, picnicking. One of my abandoned antampas separates our bodies from the neatly trimmed grass on the bare ground. The antampas is from the hundreds I got for my Kayan Lefe bridal gifts.

'Everyone will experience heartbreak,' Qub continues. 'A heartbreak so bad, that it will completely kill the mind and soul, leaving nothing but an empty and deranged soul."

I look up to my soulmate, lifting my body off his long legs. The erstwhile satisfaction of the breeze blowing my face is suddenly gone, replaced with an uncomfortable heat.

His face is in the tree branches, as though seeking out the sky. 'Where death becomes the only thing to wish for and even look forward to.' His words are thick with his Arabic accent, a coating his tongue acquired from years and years of reading the Qur'an. Suddenly, he looks down from the branches to the stream before us, then after a few seconds, his gaze finally finds me. His face bears no emotions, and his eyes are just there; expressionless.

'Baby,' I find my voice at last. The loose ends of my white scarf sway across my chubby face with the wind. 'Why are we talking about heartbreaks?'

He averts his gaze and focuses again on the stream. I can't help but notice the blankness in his hazelnut eyes. Even his full hair, brows, and beards which he takes care of like a pet wear a dullness. A silence lingers between us. The smell of curry from a nearby Indian restaurant swims in it.

The silence simmer for a while before I break it again. 'That was a little dark,' I say, adjusting the red scarf wrapped around my upper body. My long black abaya covers the other half down to my feet to shield me from mosquito bites. My dark eyebrows move even closer to form a mild frown on my face. 'Doesn't time heal a broken heart like they always say? Why's your own analysis different?'

He leans in and plants a long kiss on my forehead, his long beards brushing my eyes. 'Let's go home, babe,' he says, ignoring my questions. 'It's getting late.'

I break off from him and stare long and hard at his lips. They always know the right words to say, but they're not doing that now. Also, they always wear a smile that warms my insides, but not now. I just can't wait to leave.

I whisper to myself that I shouldn't read much into the whole scenario. So I stand up, dust myself and, together with him, I begin to pack up.

But I will soon realize I should have read deep into the scenario.

~

"Motun! Motun! Motun! Are you deaf? Where has this mind of yours drifted to again?"

I'm jolted back to my awful reality by the snarls of my mother-in-law, calling my native name as though she is my mother. My response is cloaked in reluctance: "Yes ma. I am here. What do you need?"

Hers is cloaked in bitterness. "Why haven't you made dinner yet? Or are you trying to starve us, wai? To kill us just like you killed my son? You lazy girl"

"No ma. I am not trying to starve you," I say as politely as I can, standing up from the cushioned bench before a piano. "If I wanted to kill you, I would have done that a long time ago, trust me. And as far as I am concerned, you have a cook. I suggest you go and ask him, and not me. Ma."

Her lips hung apart, but they did not make words.

"Sai Lazhin," I say goodnight in Nupe and make my way out of the main parlour without waiting for a reply. I ascend the grand stairway, headed to the master bedroom where I stay most times because Qub's mom refused to return to her husband's home since Qub left.

Mariam bint Najib is a sophisticated woman who reeks of authority. She is as hard as a brick, bitter and stuck in her ways. A Northern Muslim princess from a royal family in Niger State, she has lush, fair skin that is smooth as honey, pointed nose and squinty eyes. From afar, she seems as meek as a kitten. Her husband, Abdul Bari Ibn Kathur is the complete opposite. Soft, with a pure heart, he is a tall, dark man, with a full beard and balding head that always hides behind a tagia cap to match his crisps babariga. He is a humble and true Muslim; half Nupe and half Yoruba, from a lineage of wealth, himself the CEO of one of the country's biggest car dealerships.

Ever since I joined Ibn Kathur's family as a bride nine years ago, Mariam made it clear that she disapproved of me. I was a seventeen-year-old girl from a Yoruba home who had married her 23-year-old youngest son, Yaq'ub Ibn Bari. I was neither rich nor poor, and I had lost my mother when I was 13. To her, I was flawed in every way, and she never missed a chance to tell me. When Yaq'ub drove to our love garden, of all the places in the world, and drowned himself in the stream three years ago, she blamed me. Then she moved in against everyone's advice. Her reason: she wanted to look after me. But instead, she deprived me of the time and space I needed to grieve for my love. I have put up with her torment for too long, and I have had enough. I loved my husband. I have nothing to apologise for, at least not to her.

'Everyone will experience heartbreak. A heartbreak so bad, that it will completely kill the mind and soul, leaving nothing but an empty and deranged soul. Where death becomes the only thing to wish for and even look forward to.'

Qub's words echo in my mind as I casually lie under the duvet, hoping for sleep, one without nightmares. But I know this is merely wishful thinking.

~

I miss you. Where are you? I still go to our memory palace in search of us. The beautiful stream bank that brought us together. The one that also took you from me. I go there hoping to feel something. You know, I thought I felt you when the sunset hue fell upon me. I thought maybe I saw you looking for me, because I swear, I felt a beat. But you...you vanished again. Where have you gone to?!

I wallow with my hand probing my chest, my long fingernails—that I care less to trim—digging into my chest through my white house dress. The dress is soaked and stained from cloaking me without change for weeks now, and by the incessant stream of tears gushing from my eyes. Seated on my Ottoman bed, clutching thick super king duvet, I feel my head echoing, throbbing with blurry eyes. I see the white, furry cushion bench placed at the foot of the bed, or the white vertical cupboard seated at the left side of the room, propped up against the wall with Qub's dark swivel recliner beside it.

Qub's favorite book lay open on the table before the chair, as it has been since he left it there. I see the furry rug in the middle of the room, on which the bed cushion sits, and the bed also rests some of its frame. Qub and I decided not to have a TV in the room, so we filled the space with a big wall mirror instead. He loved the color white. It's all he wears in the images I see of him in my head now. I cry and plead at the whiteness of the walls that have entrapped Qub to please free him to me.

"Can you hear me? Where the hell are you?! You left me! Why! Answer me!" I yell as I beat drums on my chest. All this while, I've been engulfed with anger, but now I feel it tainted with a tinge of betrayal. "You belong to me! Only me! Answer me!!.... Please, I need..."

I break down into more tears. This is the loop I've been caught in since the news of your death invaded my space and stole my sanity away.

~

"Qub? What are you still doing up at this time?" I question, calling out to him from the bed, as I hear the typewriter clicking in the study. I drop my feet to the laminated floor and immediately recoil from its coldness. It's not harmattan season just yet. The AC is not on either.

"Qub?" I call out quietly, as I open the door to the study

"Qu—" I stop abruptly when I don't see him seated, even more horrified to see the typewriter still typing, clicking vigorously, making my head turn.

"Madinah."

I turn so fast I almost lost my balance, surprised I didn't get a whiplash. But I don't see him standing behind me.

"Qub? Wha... What's wrong? Wh... What's going on?" I ask with a shaky voice. And then I see him standing right in front of the open windows— windows with no barricade.

"I finished writing my story, Madinah. It's time for me to go." He says, his face contorted with apparent fright as he dangerously moves closer to the windows.

"Common Qub, what are you saying? Let's just go okay, baby?" I say. "I am here now, okay? Let's...let's go to bed, come on..." I encourage, moving slowly towards him, like going any faster will scare him, seeing just how frightened he looks.

I see the gleaming tear line on his face before I hear him crying. He's looking my way, but way past me. "It's too late, Dinah," he says, his voice quavering. "It's too late! It's here!" Beyond the tears, there's a finality in his voice, a quiet urgency that translates in my head as a frantic scream.

"What's late, Qub? What's here?"

The lights fizzle dimmer and dimmer until the moonlight outside is all that helps me to still see Qub. I'm still moving slowly but the distance between us remains the same, and the cold is more ferocious now.

My eyes suddenly catch a movement across the window pane, a bony hand dragging nails across the glass with a screeching sound. A dark shadow slowly passes by the window and suddenly disappears. "Qub? Wha...what's going on?" I cry as I turn to face him, my fear spilling into my words. But he looks just as petrified.

"I wouldn't worry about him right now, madam."

I jump, startled by the echoed voice in my head, a voice much louder than it should be. It is brought from within and a whisper fanning breath on my neck. It has a vile tone that feels like needles piercing my whole body, making me want to close my eyes, grind my teeth, and tearing out my ears while screaming to show just how violated I feel with that voice.

I turn abruptly, looking around, trying to find the voice. "Wh...who's there?" I ask, bewildered.

"You wouldn't know me, Ma Cherie." The words slam against my eardrums as though it is from a megaphone placed against my ear. "Your husband has sold himself to me. Hungry to write his story and leave this miserable world. Not even his religion could save him. Humans and greed! Time's up, Ma Cherie. I have come to claim what is mine!"

~

"Nooo!!!" I jerk up from my nightmare covered in sweat, and with tears streaming down my cheeks. My throat feels sore from the screaming, and my heart pounds like a bass drum on a parade ground.

"It was just a dream, it was just a dream," I say to myself, shaking with fear, sitting on my bed in plain darkness, trying to adjust my eyesight.

I hated sleep since everything that happened, sleep has only ever drifted me into a series of nightmares. Remembering the name I so loved hearing Qub call me—Ma Cherie—coming from that voice made my inside boil, and my heart palpitate.

The brightness of the sun soon starts to banish the night's darkness. I tiredly get up to make my bed. This morning, I will leave the tears, and my empty chest alone. I'll do my best to look alive. I put on a plain white abaya, a matching scarf, and some Arabian perfume oil. I strap on a pair of leather sandals and sling a tote bag over my shoulder. Then I snap up my sunshades; my tired eyes will feel naked without them. I am breaking my mother in-law's rule of always having my driver carry me around today. I gave him a break yesterday, now I'm going for a ride, driving myself.

Going to the gallery is the only thing I look forward to each day since Qub left. Tayarat Alhuzn (تيارات الحزن) which means 'the Streams of Sadness' is located at the heart of Abuja, in Central Business Area. It is made specially for bad memories; a safe space for people to dump their burden in a bid to help them move on. It has two sections, the first of which is painted black with illuminating white lights, it focuses on each art work display, different pieces of old art abstractly placed around the open space, with a long grey bench placed in the middle on the polished hardwood floor. The second section has the same design as the first, only painted white as a color of peace. It is a space where people bring items that have given them the courage to move on, or an achievement of moving forward. Back when Ya'qub first shared the idea of coming here, I immediately fell in love with it. My favorite part is naming it in Arabic, Ya'qub favorite language. These days, though, my attachment to the place has grown stronger. Like many other people who throng it as often as I do, I've come to see it as some sort of asylum.

When Ya'qub was alive, we would spend time in the other part of the gallery, the one that contains items of moving forward. I always hated going to the sorrowful part, but now, that is the only place I find myself, looking at all the pieces there. And today, like other days, it feels like I am drowning in the sorrows the pieces hold.

The gallery is closing for the day. I am the only one left inside, glaring at the piece that drew my Qub away from me, and away from life. The typewriter.

"What are you? What did you do? Wh...who are you" I ask the typewriter, my voice filled with sincere genuineness, as though expecting to get an answer.

"Don't you remember me, Ma Cherie?"

My heart leaps to my throat and goosebumps spread all over me. The hair on my body stands erect like the fur of a threatened cat. That voice! Isn't it meant only for my nightmares? This is not a dream, is it?

"Who the hell are you?" I ask.

"I am the holder of your dreams, of your life, of your beloved. I am the key to everything you want, Ma Cherie. Aren't you lonely, huh? Don't you miss your darling Ya'qub? I can help you feel again, help that heart beat again. You would like that now, wouldn't you?"

"Ye...yes" I whisper, clutching my gown and shaking like a junkie in need of a fix. My eyes are wide, scared, and hopeful.

"That's it, my la Cherie. You know what to do. Come to me. Go! Go and meet your beloved, where your happiness lays, la Cherie."

"Really?"

"Go Cherie, before it's too late."

"O...okay" I whisper, my legs moving as though controlled remotely by someone else. Perhaps my legs get the message. Perhaps they know this place that the voice speaks of, because my brain is no longer in control; it's completely shut down.

The ocean is always beautiful at night, dazzling with the reflection of stars, glowing with the bright colours of the city's lights. It is as tempting as a plate of food to a starved person. It's always been food, and I've always been hungry, but all this while, I have been doing my best to resist the urge.

Tonight though, the waves float so peacefully, it feels like home. This is home. I am going home.

"Ya'qub? Baby, I am coming, okay? You won't be alone anymore. It's promised that we would both be happy, together again, forever, so everything will be alright. Qub, we will be together again. I promise." I cry as I speak with each step forward. I never knew calmness and terror could exist amicably in the same body. But I'm calm and the beating of my heart mirrors my terror. Maybe it's easy because at this point, I know I already know that I am dead, soulless, just an empty vessel looking for where to perish. I strip my clothes off, ready to jump. Jump to peace and freedom.

"That's it, la Cherie, Go." It's the voice again.

Splash!!!

"Go and meet your doom."

Contributors

Aishat Adesanya is a 20-year-old Yoruba hijabi who started drawing at the age of nine. She later discovered her love for writing and published her first story at age 17. She is an avid reader and aspires to use her art and unique African culture to make a positive impact on the world. Her writing has been featured in Lion and Lilac Arts, The Journal of African Youth Literature, Hearth Magazine, and Schuylkill Valley Journal. Aishat writes from the West Midlands in the United Kingdom.

Ayo Deforge is a Nigerian writer who resides in the South of France. An alumna of the Chimamanda Adichie's Creative Writing Workshop (2007) and the Faber Academy Writing Course (2022), she has worked as a freelance writer for the Nigerian Daily Independent Newspaper and NGEX.com, and her writing has appeared in Litro Magazine, Brittle Paper, Ayo Magazine, Kalahari Review and Lucy Writers Platform (an online writing forum established by Lucy Cavendish College, University of Cambridge). She served as a reader for the Inaugural Oxbelly Writers Retreat and she teaches Read Like A Writer classes. Her debut novel, Tearless, was published in December of 2023.

Chinonso Nzeh is first Igbo, then a storyteller and photojournalist. His writing explores the intricacies of the human condition. His works have appeared in Evergreen Review, Isele Magazine, Agbowó, Maroko Journal, The Shallow Tales Review, and elsewhere. His essay, The Slipping Away, won the Isele Nonfiction Prize for 2023. He's currently studying law at the University of Lagos.

Chinuzoke Chinuwa is from Ahoada East in Rivers, Nigeria. A law graduate of Rivers State University, he is interested in the essence of storytelling in various endeavours, from social justice and climate change activism to archaeology and astronomy. He runs a *Viewbug* account for his photography and aspires to become a filmmaker. Some of his prose and poetry have been published under a pseudonym. *The Good Spirits* is his first short story to be published.

Chourouq Nasri is an associate professor in the department of English Studies at Mohamed Premier University, Oujda, Morocco. She authored numerous publications on topics related to literature, media and visual culture. She also published fiction and literary nonfiction in international anthologies and magazines. She is the author of "Anna" in ID. New Short Fiction from Africa (2018), "Outside Riyad Dahab" in Hotel Africa: New Short Fiction from Africa (2019), "A Bus Ride to Ouad Nachef" in Kohl Journal in 2019, "Wheat Thief" in Tint Journal in 2021, "Burning Bodies" in Afrocritik in 2022, and "Love, a Lens to See the World Through" in Brittle Paper in 2022.

David Ben Eke has always loved books and stories since he was a child. A native of Ekpeye land, Ahoada East, in Rivers state, Nigeria, he believes words are more than mere utterances; they are powerful vehicles of meaning that assist one in making sense of the complexities of the human experience which differ from human to human. He is keen on depicting these complexities through prose, poetry, and the hybrid forms he creates sometimes. He writes for the love of God and man, and hopes his writing stirs same. Presently, he is undertaking an LLB (Law) degree at the University of Bradford, where he serves as an Editor for the University of Bradford School of Law Journal, the Faculty of Law Representative, the President of the Athletics club, and Vice President of the Creative Writing society. His poem, 'This One Spot' was published in Olugbon Review's 'The People's Stage'.

Elisha Oluyemi has writing/interviews published or forthcoming in journals, including Strange Horizons, Lolwe, Broken Antler Quarterly, Mystery Tribune, The Bitchin' Kitsch, Isele Magazine, Brittle Paper, Terror House, Entropy Squared, Sledgehammer, Ghudsavar Magazine, and elsewhere. He writes in the psychological and literary genres. Elisha loves learning Korean, listening to classical music, and studying criminal minds.

Enit'ayanfe Ayosojumi Akinsanya is a Nigerian writer. He grew up in Sagamu, among the Yorùbá people of Nigeria. He was top finalist for the 2018 Dusty Manuscript GTB Unpublished National Novel Prize, and for the 2023 Afritondo Short Story Prize. He won the first overall position at the 2022 Itanile International Short Fiction Award and won the First-Position Prize also for the 2022 Bicontinental Arts Lounge Nonfiction Contest for "The Green We Left Behind" CNF Climate-Change Print Anthology Project. A recipient of several more national and international awards and recognitions, including Essayist of the Year at Isele Magazine, he is 29 years old. He holds a second-class upper double-honors degree in English Language and Education from Obafemi Awolowo University in Ile-Ife, Nigeria. He is the author of a short-story collection, "How to Catch a Story That Doesn't Exist". He reads poetry and watches deeply human films.

Michael Chiedoziem Chukwudera is a writer and freelance journalist. His works have appeared in Jalada Africa, Open Country, Republic, Havik, Afapinen, Afrocritik, Kalahari Review and elsewhere. He is the author of the poetry chapbook, "Painter of Love" (Heiress 2023); and the novel, "Loss is an Aftertaste of Memories" (Mmuta Books 2024). He is the director of Umuofia Arts and Books Festival which holds annually in Southeastern Nigeria.

Miracle Elvis ifesinachi is a journalist and a tech enthusiast. He studies English Literature at Obafemi Awolowo University, Osun State where he is a member of the Association of Campus Journalists. His love for storytelling has resulted in him doing so in several forms: short stories, film scripts, news reports, poetry and computer codes. He aims to raise conversations with his works around the subjects of family dynamics, hunger and the practice of faith in Africa. His works have been published on/in ARISE News Global, WE NAIJA Anthology by Nigeria Solidarity Support Fund, Shuzia "Unseen" Anthology and other platforms. He is also a lover of spoken word poetry and considers it an art form he adores but is unworthy of creating.

When he is not working or googling Marsai Martin, he attends spoken word grand slam events.

Mohammed Babajide Mohammed, a dedicated and impassioned writer, traces his love for storytelling to early childhood. For him, writing transcends a mere hobby; it's a guiding beacon in a life that was once void of direction. The pen, wielded with artistic finesse, becomes a compass navigating a sea of uncertainties, embarking on a profound journey of self-discovery. From a tender age, Mohammed finds solace and purpose in writing. His words, meticulously crafted, stand as a testament to resilience and a pathway back to belonging. Through his pen, he weaves narratives resonating with authenticity, captivating hearts. Mohammed's literary prowess extends beyond storytelling; he's a published writer, featured in "The Journal of African Youth Literature. As a writer, he leaves an indelible mark on the literary landscape, connecting profoundly with the human experience and inspiring those navigating life's complexities through the depth of his narratives.

Mustapha Enesi is a short story writer whose work explores grief, longing, sexuality and acceptance. In 2021 he won the K&L Prize for African Literature, the Awele Creative Trust Award, and he was Theme Winner for the 2021 Aster Lit Short Story Prize. He was a finalist for the 2021 Alpine Fellowship Writing Prize and the 2021 Arthur Flowers Flash Fiction Prize. One of his flash fiction pieces was published in the 2022 Best Small Fictions anthology. He has also been nominated for Best of the Net for his flash fiction piece published in Milk Candy Review and he was longlisted for the 2022 Kendeka Prize for African Literature. In 2023 he was a joint winner of the Young Writers Award for the Bridport Short Story Prize and was longlisted for the 2023 Commonwealth Short Story Prize. His works have appeared in Harvard University's Transition Magazine, Litro Magazine, The Republic, Isele Magazine, Peatsmoke Journal, The Maine Review and The Story Tree Challenge Maiden Anthology among others. He is Ebira and he writes from Lagos, Nigeria.

Obinna Inogbo is a Nigerian public relations entrepreneur who started Worktainment Limited in 2017. The company has managed the reputations of Nigerian celebrities, C-suite executives, and companies in several industries such as supply chain management, real estate, healthcare, maritime and aviation. Prior to this he worked as a TV producer and screenwriter in the Nigerian broadcasting and entertainment industry for 8 years.

Roseline Mgbodichinma is a Nigerian writer passionate about documenting women's stories. Her writing explores the intersection of nature, womanhood, emotion, bodies and desire, and how they exist and function in society. She is an alumnus of the Library of Africa and The African Diaspora (LOATAD) West African Writers Residency program. Her writing has been published in Isele, The Willowherb Review, Agbowo, SprinNG, Native Skin and elsewhere.

Thirikwa Nyingi is a teacher by profession. He lives in Laikipia county in Kenya. During his free time, he likes reading and playing chess with friends.

Witsprouts Anthologies Team includes Timileyin Okunlola, Folashade Adegoke, Mosadoluwa Fasasi, Zainab Abubakar, Sadia Aliyu, Hajara Abdul

Printed in Great Britain
by Amazon